Here'

Gemma Halliday

"A saucy combination of romance and suspense that is simply irresistible."
- Chicago Tribune

"Stylish... nonstop action...guaranteed to keep chick lit and mystery fans happy!"
- Publishers' Weekly, starred review

"Smart, funny and snappy… the perfect beach read!"
- Fresh Fiction

"If you have not read these books, then you are really missing out on a fantastic experience, chock full of nail-biting adventure, plenty of hi-jinks, and hot, sizzling romance. Can it get any better than that?"
- Romance Reviews Today

"(A) breezy, fast-paced style, interesting characters and story meant for the keeper shelf. 4 ½!"
- RT Book Reviews

OTHER BOOKS BY GEMMA HALLIDAY

High Heels Mysteries:
Spying in High Heels
Killer in High Heels
Undercover in High Heels
Christmas in High Heels (short story)
Alibi in High Heels
Mayhem in High Heels
Sweetheart in High Heels (short story)
Fearless in High Heels
Honeymoon in High Heels (short story)
out August 2012!

Hollywood Headlines Mysteries:
Hollywood Scandals
Hollywood Secrets
Hollywood Confessions

Anna Smith-Nick Dade Thrillers
Play Nice

Young Adult Books
Deadly Cool
Social Suicide

Other Works
Viva Las Vegas
A High Heels Haunting
Watching You (short story)
Confessions of a Bombshell Bandit (short story)

UNBREAKABLE BOND

GEMMA HALLIDAY

AND

JENNIFER FISCHETTO

To my daughter for the countless brainstorm sessions, even when you rolled your eyes and paid no attention. I'm lucky to have you as a best friend.

To my son for your constant encouragement and endless supply of ideas, even when I plugged my ears and screamed, "No more." Your enthusiasm is infectious. I love you more.

To my guy for all the unconditional love and support you silently bestow.

And to Mom for picking up that first book and introducing me to my imagination.

This is for all of you.

~Jennifer

For my mom, who would have dressed like Big Bird, too.

~Gemma

CHAPTER ONE

———

"Pick one."

Two eight-by-ten glossy photos dropped onto my desk.

I looked up. "Excuse me?"

Paul Levine, my weedy looking attorney, sighed, then sank into the imitation leather chair opposite my desk. "You've been running in the red for the last three months. You've got a balloon payment on the business loan coming up, and this month you pulled in fifty percent less revenue than last. Unless you want to drown in your own debt, you need to fire someone." He gestured again to the two photos. "Pick one."

I glanced down at the two pictures. A leggy brunette and an all-American-girl blonde. I shoved them back across the desk.

"No way."

Levine did another deep, theatrical sigh. "I had a feeling you'd say that."

"Look, business is just a little slow."

"It's a tortoise, Jamie."

"It's been the off season."

"There's an 'on' season for infidelity?" he asked, doing air quotes with his fingers.

"We'll take out some ads."

"Which cost money. Something, my dear, that you don't have."

I narrowed my eyes at him. "I'll think of something."

Levine leaned forward, the overhead lights shining unattractively off his bald spot. "Let's face it, people just aren't getting divorced these days. With the economy the way it is, women would rather turn a blind eye to their husbands' indiscretions than try to exist on half his income. It's cheaper to stay together and pretend to be happy."

"No one can pretend for that long."

"Pick. One," Levine enunciated.

I looked down at the two photos, which incidentally consisted of 50% percent of the Bond Agency. The problem wasn't that I'd over hired. The problem was I knew jack shit about running a business.

Men. That's what I knew.

When I was seven years old Chad Fischer's Mom packed him a Snickers bar in his lunch. And not those fun size suckers. This was a king-sized log of nougat, caramel, and sugar induced highs that would last well past the end of afternoon cartoons. I wanted it. Every kid in second grade wanted it. But I tossed my blonde hair over one shoulder, batted my baby blues at Chad, and promised that he could stand underneath me while my little pink skirt and I did flips on the monkey bars at recess. I got the Snickers. That was my first lesson in how easy men were.

Fast forward a few years, and my fifteen-year-old self was hanging out at the Northridge mall slurping a Jamba Juice when I'd been spotted by Maurcess DeLine, owner of the world renowned DeLine Models. Suddenly I wasn't just working the boys at my school; I was working every guy that bought a magazine with my body on the cover. And getting paid handsomely to do it. I'd been DeLine's top model for over a decade when Maurcess had started to drop hints that my fresh innocence act wasn't cutting it anymore. I was twenty-six. A dinosaur in runway years.

That's when I moved back to L.A. and decided to take over the family business.

Domestic espionage.

Really, there was very little difference between making love to a camera and making a married man forget his vows. In fact, this was sometimes even easier. Men with adultery already on their minds were simple targets. It was like taking Snickers from a second grader all over again.

Unfortunately, getting their wives to pay was a whole other matter.

I glanced at the two photos staring up at me. Truth was, I needed both of these women.

"Cutting back on personnel only means I can handle *fewer* cases. I don't see how that's going to help me expand the business," I argued.

"We're not talking expansion here, Jamie. We're talking staying afloat. We're talking not filing for bankruptcy."

"I've got a big client tonight. Judge Thomas Waterston. Superior court. If things go well, I guarantee his wife will have her entire bridge club in here by the end of the week."

"Well, you'd better hope that's true," Levine said, rising. "Because your balloon payment is due on the 1st. You've got two weeks, then..." He tapped the photos. "One of them's got to go."

* * *

"Caleigh?"

"What?" She swiveled in her desk chair, turning her wide eyes my way.

"You're on the Peters case. Care to give us an update?" I tapped open the schedule app on my phone and leaned an elbow across the conference table.

She cleared her throat and shuffled the notes in her lap. Caleigh Presley hailed from the south, claiming she was some distant cousin of Elvis's. Blonde, blue-eyed and bubbly, she'd cornered the market on perky. I'd met Caleigh while doing a *Sports Illustrated* swimsuit shoot in Cancun. She'd smuggled a bag of fat free Cheetos onto the set, and we'd bonded instantly. Three years later Caleigh foolishly agreed to go out on a date with Nigel Owens, the top fashion photographer in London. I say foolishly because everyone but Caleigh knew about his particular fetish for bondage and tickling. When Caleigh refused to be molested by his feather duster, Nigel had refused to work with her, calling her "difficult". News that quickly spread to other photographers, her agent, and every high profile account in the fashion world. They'd dropped her like a skydiver without a parachute. Luckily for her, that had been just about the time I'd taken over the Bond Agency, and I'd hired her on the spot.

Not, mind you, that I'd hired her out of any sort of pity. Despite her innocent-little-thing looks, Caleigh spoke five different languages and had the computer know-how to hack into the pentagon. Dumb blonde she was not.

"Right. Peters." Caleigh cleared her throat again. "Well, so far I've followed him to the Venice Boardwalk, Element, and out to dinner twice at Formaggio's."

"And?"

She shook her head. "Nothin'. I'm beginning to wonder if his wife isn't paranoid. So far the guy's a straight arrow. Both the dinners were business meetings, and he didn't so much as glance at a bikini on the boardwalk."

I picked up my coffee cup and swished the dregs around in the bottom, trying to remember if Mrs. Peters had seemed the paranoid type when she'd come in last week. Or, more importantly, the type who would balk at the amount of billable hours we'd spent with nothing to show for it. "What about the club? Element?"

Again, Caleigh shook her head. "Sorry, boss. He ducked in for a drink with a buddy, danced a little, then ducked back out. No funny business."

"Fine. If we don't have anything by Monday, we'll call it off. But take Sam with you this weekend," I said, gesturing to the woman sitting next to her, "and tag-team him. Every man has a breaking point."

Caleigh nodded and made a note on the yellow pad in her lap.

I turned to Sam. "Where are we with the Nortons?"

Samantha Cross had come to me from Brooklyn last year. Long legs, perfect mocha latte skin, and thick dark curls, Sam had been a finalist on the first season of the reality show *America's New Hot Model* and quickly become the darling of the cover girl world. Until five years later when her boyfriend, Julio, had knocked her up. As if taking a nine month hiatus from modeling hadn't been enough to kill her fledgling career, it turned out Sam wasn't one of those lucky ladies whose bodies miraculously snap back after pregnancy. While she was still a knockout among normal people, the two ounces of fat hanging around her lightly stretch-marked belly put a decisive end to her bikini days. So, Sam had packed up the munchkin (Julio was long gone at that point) and headed out to California to make a career change. One I was happy to facilitate. Sam had legs long enough to make husbands forget their vows and, thanks to her military-brat upbringing, knew more about guns than the NRA. And her aim was flawless. Sam could shoot the balls off a fruit fly at fifty yards.

"Mrs. Norton's lawyer," Sam said, "has requested all of our notes."

"Which we will gladly copy for him. Mrs. Norton has gone through three husbands with the agency. What Mrs. Norton wants, we give."

"Of course." Sam nodded. "I think Mr. Norton's lawyers are close to a settlement." Her brown eyes lit up, and she leaned in close. "They offered a 60/40 split plus the house in Aspen."

"Good for her." She deserved it. Especially after her husband had offered to pay Sam fifty dollars for a blow job in the back of his Jag. Sam had been so insulted that he'd offered less than a hundred, she'd actually hauled off and punched him. I made a note in my organizer to edit that part out before handing the footage over to Mrs. Norton's lawyers.

"Okay, so get the Norton files to her lawyer, then work Mr. Peters with Caleigh."

Sam nodded. "Will do."

"So… new cases this week?" I asked, turning to the woman on my left.

Maya Alexander handled all of the admin for the agency, including scheduling appointments with prospective clients. And if her face looked a little familiar, it was because she was March's Playmate of the month. Lucky for me, not many men recognized her with her clothes on.

"Uh-huh. Two possible new cases. Mrs. Shankmann, who claims her husband, and I quote, 'shtupped the freakin' au pair,' and a Rachel Blake who wants us to test her fiancée before the wedding."

Caleigh raised her hand and bounced in her seat. "Oh, me, me. I love doing bachelor parties."

"Done." I noted it down. "I'll take Mr. Shankmann if we get the account. Right. On to tonight. Judge Waterston."

All three girls leaned forward in their seats.

"We all know how high profile, i.e. high dollar, this account is."

Three heads nodded.

"So, this needs to go off flawlessly. Mrs. Waterston is a big name. She has big friends, who all have big cash on the line should they decide they need our services to bust their pre-nups."

"We're hitting him at the party?" Sam asked, checking her notes.

"Black tie benefit at the Beverley Hilton. So, I want everyone to look sharp, okay?"

Again with the nods.

"I'm personally running game on this one. Sam, you're camera one. Caleigh, I want you on two. Danny will direct from the van." I paused. "Girls, we need this guy. We can't fuck it up."

I didn't add because without him, one of them was looking at unemployment.

CHAPTER TWO

———

The Beverly Hilton is located on Wilshire in the part of Los Angeles where Mercedes outnumber homeless people fifty to one. An iconic piece of Hollywood history, the hotel has played host to countless stars, dignitaries, and legends, and holds over one hundred red carpet events each year.

And tonight's affair did not disappoint.

The plush banquet room was decorated in tactful hues of red and gold, accentuated by floral arrangements at every column. A jazz group played in the corner, creating mellow mood music for the hundred-some guests in suits and subdued cocktail dresses, nibbling at their fat-free hors d'oeuvres.

Caleigh stood to the right of the band, wearing a strapless emerald green number. In the center of her bodice sat a jade colored brooch, pointed straight at me. Sam was directly across the room from her, wearing a tight red mini-dress with a silver brooch of her own attached to her right shoulder strap. She held a glass of chardonnay in one hand and swayed slightly to the rhythm of the upright bass.

I leaned against the bar, ignoring the jab of my Glock strapped to my thigh, and lifted a single olive martini to my lips to disguise their movement. "Tell Sam I'll be intercepting the target to her right, near the front entrance," I murmured into my décolletage.

"You got it," a voice sounded in my earpiece.

I waited two beats, then Sam changed her position ever so slightly, shifting to face the entrance.

"She's got a clear shot," piped my earpiece.

"Thanks, Danny."

"Anytime, boss," he replied. Then, "Shit. Incoming at two o'clock, Jamie."

I turned to my left...

But was too late to avoid the guy in the Brooks Brothers suit with "hook-up" written all over his tanned face.

"Hi there," he said, suddenly well inside my personal space.

I took an instinctive step back, giving him a quick once over.

His hair was cropped close in a conservative style, blond, gelled into place. Green eyes, creased just a little at the corners. Broad shoulders that spoke of either high school football or a dedicated personal trainer. Not bad looking, but polished to a high sheen. In fact, if my name were Barbie, I'd say he was the perfect catch.

I gave him a semi-polite "kiss off" smile.

"Nice party, huh?" he persisted.

"Sure."

"I just moved here recently. I tell you, they don't have parties like this where I'm from."

I nodded. Sipped my drink. Prayed he'd go away.

"You from around here?" he asked.

Again, I gave the noncommittal nod.

"Well, I gotta say, the weather out here is fantastic. Sunny and seventy year round. Paradise."

Jesus, was this guy seriously trying to pick me up with talk about the weather? I'd seen better game from a ten year old.

Danny piped up in my ear. "Detach the suit, Jamie. Our mark just walked in."

I whipped my head around to the entrance. A balding, sixty-ish man stood in the doorway. Dark suit, navy tie, sharp eyes. Almost immediately a young guy with "future politician" stamped all over his pinstriped jacket was on the judge like pumps on a prostitute, jiggling his hand up and down.

"Excuse me," I said, setting my martini on the bar and turning to go.

"Aiden Prince." Brooks Brothers stuck a hand out to bar my way.

I paused. Then quickly shook it.

"And you?"

"What?" I glanced over his shoulder. The judge had detached the eager beaver. He was alone. Perfect.

"Your name?"

"Oh. Uh, Jamie. Jamie Smith." At least tonight.

He smiled, showing off a row of perfectly bleached teeth. "It's a pleasure to meet you, Jamie Smith. Can I buy you a drink?"

I pointed to the martini, still virtually untouched. "Got one, thanks. Now if you'll excuse me-"

"Here." He shoved a cocktail napkin at me, a phone number hastily scrawled on it beneath the name, "Aiden."

"My number. You know, just in case you feel like playing tour guide for the new guy some evening." He grinned.

I'll admit, the "new kid in town" thing was kinda cute.

Unfortunately, I didn't have time for cute. Out of the corner of my eye I could see the judge moving toward a group of men smoking cigars on the balcony. It was now or never.

"Thanks," I mumbled and shoved the napkin into my cleavage.

Danny piped up in my ear again as I threaded my way through the growing crowd. "I thought that guy would never give up."

"You and me both," I mumbled.

"There he is," Danny directed. "Near the French doors."

"I'm on it. Sam's in position?" I asked.

"She's right behind you."

I quickly glanced over my shoulder to see the brunette keeping pace three feet behind.

"Then it's show time."

* * *

I stared at the "new voicemail" alert on my cell, trying to ignore it.

Last night had gone off without a hitch. So well, in fact, that after reviewing the footage with Danny, he'd taken off for an early morning shoot in Malibu, and the girls and I had gone out for mojitos to celebrate. Until two a.m. The resulting headache this morning was a cruel reminder that I was no longer twenty-one. And the last thing that mixed well with a killer hangover was an early morning chat with *him*.

I shoved my cell into my bag.

Maya popped her head into my office. "You want to go over your schedule for the day?"

I grunted in the negative.

She set a large Starbucks cup down on my desk. "How about now?"

"I love you." I grabbed the cup, gratefully taking a sip. It was so hot it burned my tongue. Perfect. "Okay, hit me."

Maya recited the appointment book from memory. "You've got an eleven-thirty phone conference with Mrs. Chen's lawyer – they're withholding payment. Mr. Chen's lawyer said the footage was too blurry to clearly make out Mr. Chen's face."

I rubbed my temples. "Fabulous."

"You have Maguire this afternoon, and the landlord called about the rent check. Apparently," Maya averted her eyes, "it bounced."

I cringed, trying not to picture Levine's pinched face as he wagged his proverbial finger at me. "I'll take care of it. Anything else?"

"Mrs. Waterston is waiting in reception."

I nodded. "Give me two minutes, then show her in."

"Okay. Oh, and, uh," she bit her lip. "Derek left two messages here last night."

"I figured. He left one on my cell, too."

"Do you want me to call him back?" Maya asked, even though I could tell she dreaded it as much as I did.

"No, I'll call him later," I said. At least halfway meaning it. "But thanks."

Maya's face brightened, visibly relieved. "Okay. Two minutes then," she said, then left.

I drank the rest of my coffee as I pulled Mrs. Waterston's file from my bottom drawer. It was, admittedly, slim. My typed report on the evening, a couple of blown up stills – eight by tens always added more drama when it came time to negotiate settlement terms – and the copy of the footage Danny had shot last night. Then I opened a fresh box of tissues and set it on the corner of my desk.

Just in case.

I popped Danny's disk into my computer and pulled up the media player just as Mrs. Waterston came into the room.

"Good morning, Miss Bond." Her voice was soft and evenly modulated, hinting just the slightest of an indefinable upper-crust accent. It reminded me of an old Hepburn movie, and I wondered if it was natural or carefully cultivated.

She was young, slim, the obvious trophy wife. While her husband had spent one too many nights in the pursuit of cigars, scotch, and blondes, his wife looked to prefer spending her time at the spa, the salon, and cruising Rodeo. She wore a simple cashmere twin set and dark slacks, nervously twisting her hands together in front of her.

"Mrs. Waterston, please have a seat," I said, gesturing to the chair opposite my desk.

"Thank you. You have something I can take to my lawyers?" she asked, the tension in her stiff posture almost palpable.

I put on my best sympathetic voice. Which wasn't very hard. After one evening with Judge Grabby Hands, I had enormous sympathy for anyone who'd had to endure him for years. "Yes, I'm afraid we do."

She nodded. "Alright, let's have it."

I nodded, hitting "play".

As the video began, she sat silently, both hands clasped in her lap. Behind her poker face I had no idea what she was thinking, but she didn't move a muscle.

I watched myself sidle up to Judge Waterston on the screen. I giggled, touched his arm. He offered to buy me a drink, leaned in just a little too close. It didn't take long before his hand found its way to my thigh, and he was propositioning me for a private evening of hide the gavel.

"I've got a room upstairs," I heard myself respond. "Three-eighteen. Don't disappoint me." I slid off my stool with practiced seductiveness, and Sam got the perfect shot of the judge grabbing my ass as I walked away.

Then the screen went blank.

I cleared my throat, trying to clear the awkward silence from the room with it.

"I'm sorry. I know this must be hard to watch."

"Yes, it is," she agreed. She looked down, picking at invisible lint on the arm of her chair. Her face was pale and placid, but I was glad, at least, there weren't any tears. I hated tears.

"If there's anything I can do?" I said, leaving the vague offer hanging.

"No, thank you, Miss Bond. You've done enough." She opened her clutch and slipped on a pair of small, calfskin driving gloves, before pulling out a matching wallet. "What do I owe you for your services?"

"We'll send you a bill later. You don't have to worry about that now."

"No, I'd prefer to pay now, if you don't mind."

I nodded. Hey, if writing a check helped her work out her grief, who was I to argue? "Then Maya will give you a balance."

"Thank you." Mrs. Waterston stood up and stuck out one small hand. I shook it, her gloves soft and cool against my palm.

"The disk." She gestured to my computer. "May I have a copy of that?"

"Of course. You can take this one." I popped the disk out and handed it over to her. "Again, I'm sorry."

Mrs. Waterston slipped it into her clutch and stood up. "No need to be. I've known he was a cheating bastard for years. I thank you for finally giving me the proof I need to bury the man." She paused and smiled at me. "In court, that is. Thank you again, Miss Bond. It's been a pleasure doing business with you."

With that, she turned and strode into the reception area, where she paused only briefly to speak with Maya, then handed over her balance in cash. Which was no big surprise. Most of the women who came in here didn't want their husband finding a charge to a P.I. firm on their monthly credit card or bank statements. Cash was the common payment. Don't worry, I reported every cent to the IRS.

I watched as Mrs. Waterston took her receipt, then walked out the frosted front doors, painted with the single word "Bond" in bold black letters.

CHAPTER THREE

———

"Derek called this morning."

Danny looked across the table at me. "And?"

"Five times. He called *five* times. Somehow I get the feeling he doesn't trust me." I paused. "He thinks I'm too girly to do this job."

Danny grinned, a crooked thing that made the corners of his eyes crinkle, then let his gaze slowly rove my person, taking in my silk blouse, pencil skirt, and pink high heeled pumps. "Newsflash. You *are* girly."

I threw a tortilla chip across the table at him.

We were at Bosco's Cantina, a hole-in-the wall place near the beach, munching on chips and salsa while waiting for Maguire to make his appearance. According to the man's wife, he was always "at the gym" lately. According to his credit card statement, a dozen roses had been delivered to the pink apartment building across the street last month. To a Miss Lula LaRue. It didn't take a rocket scientist to figure out what kind of "work outs" Maguire had been engaging in.

"So, how was the Malibu shoot this morning?" I asked Danny, loading a chip with chunky salsa.

"Hot." He leaned back in his chair, clasping his hands behind his head, a gesture that stretched out all 6'2" of him.

I'd met Danny on my first professional photo shoot when I was fifteen - all gangly legs, and scared shitless at the thought of standing in front of all those cameras in nothing but my itty bitty bikini. He'd immediately stepped into the role of big brother, putting me at ease and showing me the poses that made my ugly ducking shape instantly resemble a swan. The pictures had been good enough to get me a three page layout in *Seventeen*, and we'd been friends ever since.

Though I never actually asked his age, I figured Danny was somewhere in his early forties. Old enough that fine laugh lines creased his eyes, but still young enough to pull off that rugged California guy thing. Natural outdoor tan, light brown sun-streaked hair, just a little too shaggy to be fashionable, if, in fact, too-shaggy weren't the current fashion. And exotic pale eyes, sort of an indistinguishable color somewhere between blue and green depending on the light. He'd once told me he got into photography to meet chicks, and I can't remember a time when Danny didn't have a bulging little black book.

"Malibu was hot," he repeated. "The sun was shinning, the water was clear, and the bikinis were tiny. Heaven."

I rolled my eyes. "It's all about the bikinis for you men, isn't it?"

"That's what keeps you in business, babe." Danny popped a chip in his mouth. "Speaking of which, how'd the footage from last night work?"

"Perfect. The judge is toast."

"It was the dress. You were smokin' in the dress."

"Thank you. I thought so, too."

"You give it to the wife?"

"This morning."

He lifted his beer in the air. "Then cheers to a job well done."

I lifted my water glass and clanked against the side of his bottle.

"So," Danny said, eyeing me as he took a slow, deliberate sip. "Last night. What did you do with the number?"

"What number?"

"The one Ken Doll slipped you. Got the feeling he thought you were pretty smokin' too."

"Seriously?" I pinned him with a look. "I tossed it. The guy was hitting on girls at a charity event. How hard up is he?"

"Huh." Danny picked his camera up off the table and lifted it to his eye, shooting off a couple pictures of the peeling pink paint across the street.

I hated it when he did that. Masking his expression with photographic equipment was conversation-cheating as far as I was concerned.

I nudged him with my foot. "'Huh' what? What's the 'huh' supposed to mean?"

He kept shooting as he answered. "Nothing. I just thought he looked like your type."

Oh, this was going to be good. "And exactly what type would that be?"

He shrugged, setting the camera down on the table between us. "Polished, *GQ*, hair sprayed into place with lacquer."

"Hey, it moved when he nodded."

Danny grinned.

"And, I'll have you know, that is so *not* my type."

"Oh yeah?" He leaned both elbows on the table and trained his eyes – green now in the bright afternoon sun – on me. "What is your type then, Bond?"

Luckily, I've known Danny long enough that I didn't take the bait. "I'll let you know when I see it," I mumbled instead, lifting my drink to my lips.

"Good." Danny leaned back in his seat. "Then I still have a chance."

I threw another tortilla chip at him.

"Soooo," I said, drawing out the word, "tell me more about your bikini shoot. Did *you* get a phone number?" For those of you paying attention, yes, that was my attempt at a clever conversation change.

Danny got a wicked look in his eyes. The same one that the pirated-out Johnny Depp had in Maya's screensaver at the office. Total ravage and plunder.

"Numbers. Plural." He held up two fingers, his grin stretching.

"Never mind. You've told me enough."

"I think they were twins. And, man, were they a flexible pair. The one could wrap both legs around her-"

"You are *such* a pig."

"I'm a pig, you're girly - we're the perfect pair."

A glimpse of blue metal flashed over Danny's shoulder, and I sat up in my chair as Maguire's vintage Mustang pulled up in front of the apartment building.

"Oh yeah? Well, watch and learn, Porky. This is how Girly gets her mark."

Danny swiveled in his seat just in time to see Maguire – tall, wide, and all veiny muscles - slip into the third unit on the bottom row. I threw a twenty on the table, Danny grabbed his camera, and we sprinted across the street.

"I'll take the back," I called over my shoulder as Danny slid with his back against the wall toward the third door. He nodded once, then aimed his camera at the front window.

Trying to do a mix of nonchalance and speed, I rounded the corner of the building, counting the tiny, fenced-in patios until I found Maguire's gal's. With a quick look over my shoulder, I hiked up my skirt and hoisted myself up and over the fence, landing on a cracked cement patio that looked into the back rooms of the apartment. A sliding glass door with a ripped screen led into the living room. Next to it was a high window emitting tell-tale moaning sounds.

"Right there, baby," a woman's voice encouraged.

Maguire grunted in response.

I slipped a slim digital camera from my pocket and stepped on tip-toe, lifting my lens just above the window sill.

Maguire was naked, his steroid pumped ass pounding into an African American woman in a pink negligee.

"That's it, do it to me, baby," she moaned.

I popped off a series of shots in rapid succession. This was almost too easy. I shifted under the window, getting three more incriminating photos of full frontal Maguire, and was just about to slink away and do a victory dance when a car horn sounded somewhere behind me.

And Maguire looked up.

Our eyes locked for a full two seconds before the light bulb moment hit him, and his face contorted with rage.

"Oh. Shit."

I shoved the camera in my pocket, and ran for the fence, grabbing on and hoisting myself up as adrenaline surged from

my belly. I had one leg over before Maguire's naked form burst
through the back door.

"Give me that camera, bitch!"

I quickly pulled the other leg up, dropping with a thud on
the other side and took off running.

But unfortunately, since I wasn't hopped up on muscle
juice, Maguire was a whole lot faster. Three strides into it, he
caught me, pouncing from behind.

"Uhn!" I fell forward from the force, scraping my hands as I
hit the pavement.

"My fuckin' wife send you?" he spat out as he flipped me
over. He straddled me, his beefy hands pinning my wrists to the
ground.

I pushed against his weight, but there was no way I was
winning this wrestling match. I wriggled underneath his bulk,
twisting my head to the side to avoid his hot breath on my face. I
pushed up against his hands, causing him to shift his weight
forward as he continued to pin me. I pushed up again. Once
more… then quickly slid both arms straight down to my sides.
Predictably, his body pitched forward, face first. I lifted my
forehead with a jerk and head-butted him in the nose.

"Hell!" he yelled. Blood oozed from his nostrils, stunning
him, his hands immediately flying to his face. I took the
opportunity to kick my right leg upward and over his, flipping
him onto his back. Then sent a swift knife-hand chop to his neck,
hitting his carotid artery.

I stood up and quickly backed away as he gasped for breath,
wheezing like a sick animal.

As I labored to get my own panic-fueled breathing back
under control, Danny jogged around the side of the building.

Gotta love the man's timing.

"Hey, you okay?" he asked.

"Yeah." I glanced down at my silk blouse. An ugly red stain
was spreading down the front. "But he ruined my shirt."

Danny looked from me to Maguire, concern quickly melting
into a smile as he shook his head. "Jesus, I can't take you
anywhere, Bond."

* * *

After an afternoon with Maguire I needed a long, hot shower and a drink. Not necessarily in that order.

Unfortunately, as soon as I got home I realized I had racked up two more voicemails from Derek.

I dropped onto my sofa with a sigh. I thought about ignoring them, but sadly, knowing Derek, that wouldn't make him go away. Instead, I reluctantly keyed my pin number into the voicemail system.

"Hey, it's me," came the first one, dated last night. "Just checking in. How'd things go with the judge? Call me."

I hit delete.

Even though Derek had officially retired to his houseboat last year after being shot in the shoulder by a married father of three caught with a Russian hooker in North Hollywood, he still wanted a report on every mark. I'd like to think it was because fishing in Marina Del Rey wasn't enough to occupy the mind of a twenty-seven year veteran of the P.I. business and not because he thought I needed checking up on.

That's what I'd *like* to think.

"Me again." Derek's voice filled my apartment as the second message clicked on. "Aren't you back yet? What the hell is taking so long? This was an in-and-out case, James; don't tell me you're still working him? It's nine-fifteen for Christ's sakes. I'd have had him in twenty minutes. Call me."

I gave my phone the finger.

The next few messages followed in similar fashion, growing increasingly pissed.

I deleted them all and crossed to the kitchen, pulling out a white egg timer.

When I was seventeen and doing a shoot for *French Vogue* in Cannes, I'd been stupid enough to try a line of coke an over-friendly photographer had offered. I'd ended up in the emergency room, not because of the coke, but because my high alter ego had suddenly thought herself invincible and dove off the top tier of a yacht into the Mediterranean in the middle of the night. I'd broken two ribs and smashed my face into the rotor, which left me bruised beyond the help of airbrushing for a month. My agent had been furious. He'd sent me to therapy to make sure this kind of "self destructive behavior" never dented his bank account again.

The therapy, honestly, hadn't been all that bad. Having someone actually look at me for me and not as a clothes hanger was a novelty, and it had been nice to talk to someone who was required to at least pretend to listen to me. Unlike Derek.

The best advice I'd taken away from the therapy was to set limits when I talked to Derek. Take him in small doses. Hence, the egg timer.

I wound the timer up for five minutes, took a deep breath, and dialed his number.

It rang six times, and I was just about to give up when a woman's voice answered.

"Yell-o?" she called. Followed by a cigarette stained giggle.

"Is Derek in?"

"Who's askin'?" Her accent was part Valley Girl and part trailer park, and I could hear a muffled male voice in the background.

"Jamie."

"Well, Jamie, Derek is otherwise occ-u-pied," she drew out the word. Then there was more muffled noise, followed by a swatting sound and a high pitched, "Oh, you naughty boy."

I took another deep breath, inhaling patience. As much as I wanted to hang up now, I knew it would only mean three more messages by tomorrow.

"Would you please tell Derek that his *daughter* is on the line?"

The giggling stopped. "He didn't tell me about no daughter."

"He never does," I murmured more to myself than Derek's shocked flavor of the month.

I heard the phone being handed off, then Derek's voice. "James, is that you?"

"Unless you have another daughter."

"Nothing's been proven yet."

"Ha ha. Very funny."

"Hey, cut the old man some slack, huh?"

"You left me six messages?" I prompted, hoping to get this over with.

"Is that all it takes to get my daughter to call me back these days? Just six."

"I was feeling generous."

"So, how did the judge thing go?" I could hear him popping something in his mouth. Probably Cap'n Crunch, knowing Derek. "Got anything yet? You know, James, you gotta move fast with these high profile clients. They expect instant gratification, if you know what I mean."

"Things went fine with the judge. We nailed him last night."

"Hey, good for you, pal. So, which one of the Bond Girls did you end up taking with you? That blonde one? God, she's hot."

I tilted my head to the side, and checked my timer. Three minutes left.

Shit.

Don't get me wrong, I love my dad. Honest. In fact, I'd venture to say there wasn't a woman in all of L.A. County that hadn't at one time or another fallen in love with Derek Bond. Think L.A.'s answer to Magnum P.I. Laid back, charming, and a real man's man. Unfortunately I'm a girl's girl, so you can see where we butted heads.

Plus, there was the fact that, hoping I'd come out a bouncing baby boy, Derek had named me James. James Bond. Yeah, I know. How do you forgive a guy for something like that?

"She has a name, Derek. It's Caleigh. And, yes, I took both her and Sam."

"Which one's Sam? The one with the legs?"

"They all have legs."

"Yeah, but not like hers, honey."

I looked at the timer. Two-thirty. "Don't you have company to entertain, Derek?"

"You wouldn't be trying to get rid of your dear old dad, would you?"

"Heaven forbid."

"All right, all right, I'll let you go, James. Just tell me who you're working tomorrow?"

"Shankman. Married seven years. Doing the nanny. We're sitting on the place during his lunch break."

"We?"

"I'm taking Danny."

Derek paused, silence overtaking the other end of the line. "I don't trust him, James."

"His photos are excellent, and you know it."

"I didn't say his pictures were bad. I said I didn't trust the man. He's a player."

"Takes one to know one," I mumbled.

"What was that?"

"Nothing. Listen, Derek, I can handle Danny. I'm a big girl. I'm a trained professional, remember?"

"I'll go with you."

"No!" I jumped up from the sofa, banging my shin on the coffee table. "Ow! Shit."

"What was that?"

"Nothing," I mumbled rubbing my leg. I could feel an unattractive lump growing there already. "Look, I'm doing Shankman at noon. I'm taking Danny. *You* are staying home with Miss Tricks there, and if you don't, so help me God, I'll call Dr. Pederson and remind him you haven't had your annual rectal yet."

Derek chomped down hard on a Cap'n Crunch nugget. "Oh that was a low blow, James."

"Hey, a girl's gotta do what a girl's gotta do."

"Fine. But call me when you nail him. And I mean it this time!" he shouted, then hung up on me.

Just as the egg timer buzzed.

That's it, I *really* needed a drink.

* * *

After I'd counted to ten, done a couple calming yoga breaths, and popped the top on a Corona, I flipped the TV on and walked over to the windows, staring out at the valley below me.

When I'd moved here from New York three years ago, I'd instantly fallen in love with this apartment, not because of its size – lord knows the twelfth floor loft was one step up from a shoe box – but because of the windows. They spanned the entire back side of the open room, laying all of Hollywood sprawled out in front of me. On particularly clear days, of which I admit there are few below the smog level, I could see all the way from my point in Studio City almost to the ocean.

As I drank in the view I vaguely heard the newscaster ramble on from the TV about two shootings in Compton and the fact it was going to be another scorching July day in the triple digits tomorrow, but I tuned it all out. Instead, I watched as the last remnants of day disappeared behind the horizon, painting the sky a pale, dusky blue. One by one, twinkling lights began dotting the landscape, anonymous beacons replacing the fading shadows of palm trees and billboards. I closed my eyes, letting the day melt away.

Until I heard the television spit out a familiar name.

"... breaking news about Judge Thomas Waterston."

I turned just in time to see the judge's picture flash across the screen. In two quick strides I was across the room, grabbing the remote and upping the volume.

"I repeat, this is breaking news, Tom," the young, Hispanic newscaster said into her microphone.

"Do the police have any idea how long ago this may have happened?" a male voice, presumably Tom, responded off camera.

The reporter shook her head. "No. The police are being very cautious at this point about what information they release as this is breaking news."

"What is breaking news?" I demanded of the screen.

"Do they have any leads so far?"

Again she shook her bobbed head. "They are talking to witnesses who saw the judge at a charity fundraiser last night, but beyond that, we really don't have much information at this point, Tom."

The fundraiser? I felt the Corona burning in my empty stomach. Mixing with a sensation that felt a lot like dread.

The screen switched back to the newsroom, training on a man sitting behind the anchor desk in a dark suit.

"Thank you, Soledad," he said with a practiced look of concern. "Once again, for those of you just tuning in..."

I leaned forward and turned the volume up again.

"...the body of Judge Thomas Waterston has just been found at the Beverly Hilton hotel. Police confirm that he died from a gunshot wound to the head."

I stared openmouthed at the screen. Holy shit.

The wife killed him.

CHAPTER FOUR

———

I muted the TV and lunged for the phone, dialing Danny's number. Voicemail. Dammit. Probably out with the Gumby girls. I hung up and dialed Levine.

He picked up on the first ring.

"Holy shit, Jamie, what's going on over there?"

"I take it you saw the news?"

"Saw it? I've had three heart attacks in the last five minutes. *This* was your big client? What the hell happened?" Levine demanded.

"I don't know. I guess she shot him."

"The wife?"

I nodded at the air. "Oh this is bad isn't it?"

"Well it certainly isn't good." Levine mumbled a few choice swear words under his breath. "We may be in the red, but taking on psycho clients isn't the answer, Jamie."

"For your information the wife was perfectly sane when she left my office," I shouted back.

"Yes, yes she was. That's your story, and you better damn well stick to it. God, Jamie, this is huge."

No shit. I took a deep breath. "I can't believe this. I can't believe I got someone killed."

My lawyer paused. Then his voice came slowly and deliberately on the other end. "Don't ever say those words again. Ever. You hear me?"

I nodded in compliance.

"She was a client. You did the job she hired you to do. When she left your office, you had no idea where she was going, or what her intentions were. Your professional responsibility terminated the moment she left you. Got it?"

I nodded again.

"Got it!?"

"I'm nodding."

"What do the police think?"

"I don't know. News says no one's talking yet. The media's going to be relentless on this one, though."

"Then you better talk to the wife before she talks to them," he countered. "What the wife did after she left your office, she did of her own free will. But if she so much as breathes the name Bond to anyone, we're sunk. This goes way beyond firing an employee or two. This is testifying in a murder trial, police combing through our records, press up our asses. This is not the kind of publicity we need."

"Right." I nodded at my empty apartment again.

"How did she pay?" Levine continued.

"Cash"

"She have a lawyer involved?"

"No."

"Records?"

"I gave her the disk."

"If she's smart, she's destroyed it. You have her sign a confidentiality agreement?"

I sat down on the sofa, the game of rapid fire twenty questions suddenly zapping my energy. "You know I *always* do."

"Good," he responded, and I could hear him sipping at something. Probably a double scotch. God, I wished I had something stronger than Corona in the house. "Remind her it goes both ways," Levine said. Then paused. "Quickly." And he hung up.

I swallowed down that growing ball of dread and followed Levine's instructions, immediately dialing the number Mrs. Waterston had given me. No answer. I prayed that didn't mean she was in the county detention and left a cryptic message with a lot of "call me back"s in it. After I hung up, I called Maya and left her a message giving her the heads up and telling her that should anyone from the press call, we had no comment and should anyone from the LAPD show up, make sure to ask for a warrant. I left messages with both Caleigh and Sam saying much the same. Then I called Danny again. Still no answer. Of all nights, he had to pick this one to spend with twins.

Asshole.

When I ran out of people to call, I opened my media player and cued up the video from last night again. I sat back on my leather sofa and watched it, silently sipping my third (or was it fourth?) Corona as I scrutinized my every word. It was a standard decoy play. I hadn't offered sex for money. I hadn't brought the wife along. And I hadn't made any threats whatsoever against the judge's person even when he squeezed my ass like he was testing cantaloupes. Legally, there was nothing I could be cited for.

Morally, however, I couldn't shake the feeling that I'd just gotten a man killed. Not the greatest man that ever lived, but a human being nonetheless.

I leaned my head back against my sofa cushions, and conjured up the image of Mrs. Waterston's perfect Hepburn face as she'd watched the footage just that morning. She'd seemed upset, but not overly so. Disappointed, but not angry. Sad, but not surprised. Nothing to indicate she was so unhinged as to actually kill the man.

I watched the muted TV, a scene of the coroner's van pulling up to the hotel.

Apparently I knew men, but I had a lot to learn about women.

* * *

I pulled the trigger three times, popping off each round with a satisfying jolt that rippled through my outstretched arms. A Glock 27 isn't the biggest or baddest of guns. It's not made for show, and it doesn't pack as much of a recoil as, say, a .44 Magnum. But I like it. It's sleek, small enough to fit in my purse, and packs enough of a punch that I can feel every shot vibrate through my body, from my index fingers, curled around the smooth trigger, to my toes, encased in pointy, snakeskin pumps, planted at shoulder width as I aimed for the target fifty feet away.

I pulled back, easing two more bullets down the lane, hearing the satisfying pop of them leave the barrel even through the thick padded ear coverings that were standard issue at Cisco's Range.

I lowered my weapon and hit the red button mounted beside me on the mortared safety wall. A sheet of paper bearing a head and shoulders target raced towards me from the end of the lane. Once it was close enough, I checked my accuracy. One shot to the head, two in the torso, and two more near the shoulder. Not bad. The shoulder shots would likely piss a guy off more than stop him in his tracks, but my first shot had been the head wound, so by that time the shoulders would be a moot point.

I pulled the target down and clipped a fresh sheet of paper to the line before sending it back to its position at the far end of the shooting gallery.

After spending a sleepless night haunted by images of Judge Waterston's pudgy face, his wife's perfect twinset, and a big red hole in the judge's forehead, I'd awoken cranky, exhausted, and needing to release some nervous energy. In short, I wanted to shoot something. I briefly considered targeting the phone when, after three more tries, Danny still wasn't picking up. But since my entire life was programmed into my phone, I opted for a morning at the gun range instead.

"Hey, that was pretty good," Sam shouted from the next lane over, gesturing to the mutilated target. "Three of those would have been deadly."

"Thanks," I responded. Though, I think she was just trying to make me feel better about the four shots that had gone wide and missed the guy altogether. I glanced at her target. Seven shots to the head. All in a neat little circular pattern. What did I tell you? The woman was an animal.

"So, any luck with Peters yet?" I asked her.

I watched as she squinted one eye behind her thick safety goggles, aiming at the paper man again. "No," she shouted. "I'm telling you, the man is clean. I went with Caliegh yesterday."

"And?"

"We feigned car trouble outside his office. Caleigh even wore that little denim skirt, the one that's frayed up to her butt cheeks. And you wanna know what Peters did?"

"Tell me."

"He called triple A for us, waited 'til a tow came, then wished us a pleasant evening and left. Not even a whisper of a pass at either one of us."

"I'm starting to think you're losing your touch, girl."

"I'm startin' to think the man's gay!" Sam popped off five more shots.

"Well, leave him to Caleigh for now. I want you to take over with Shankman. You're watching his place at noon with Danny."

"I thought *you* wanted this guy?"

I shook my head. "I think I'm going to lay low for a while."

She paused. "The judge thing?"

I nodded.

"Sucks," she offered.

"I'm aware."

"But it's not like it's your fault. The wife's the one that shot him, right?"

"Shh," I cautioned. Mornings at Cisco's meant trigger happy soccer moms and off duty police officers. The moms I didn't worry about so much. The cops, however, didn't exactly take talk of shooting someone lightly.

But Sam didn't give up. "You talked to Levine yet?"

I fired off three more rounds. All wild. "I can handle this. We'll be fine."

"Uh-huh." Only she didn't sound convinced.

"I called him last night," I conceded.

"And? What did he say?"

"He said our professional responsibility ended the moment she left our office. We're fine."

"Uh-huh." Again with the unconvinced thing.

And unfortunately, I wasn't in a real reassuring mood.

Instead, I smacked the red button, reeling my paper victim back in. A little better this time. Five rounds in the chest, two to the head.

I flipped the safety back on my gun and slipped it into my shoulder holster beneath my jacket.

Sam took her ear coverings off, shaking out her dark curls. "I don't know why you have to wear that thing," she said, gesturing to my gun. "It's like a hundred degrees outside, and you gotta wear a jacket to cover it."

I looked down. A fine sheen of sweat was already dotting the inside of my blazer. "I don't mind."

"Mind? You're gonna get heat stroke."

I put my hands on my hips. "Did you put on panties this morning, Sam?"

She grinned. "Are you hitting on me, boss?"

Only I'm pretty sure the look on my face told her I wasn't kidding.

"Yes," she said, "I'm wearing panties. Lacey, red ones, if you must know."

"Right, because even if no one sees them, and you don't really need them, you feel naked without them."

Sam shook her head. "Okay, I get it, boss. Insurance, huh?"

I nodded. "Something like that."

"And just for the record, sometimes, my panties do get seen." She winked. "I got a life, you know."

"TMI, Sam." I grabbed my purse, making for the exit.

"Hey," Sam called after me. "So, what are we gonna do about the judge?"

"*We* are going to do nothing. *You* are going to nail Shankman," I said, pointing a finger at her. "And *I* am gonna go talk to the wife and make sure she keeps her pretty little mouth shut."

* * *

As soon as I stepped outside I dialed Mrs. Waterston again. And got no answer, my call going straight to voicemail. Again. I left another message, asking her to *please* call me back, and hit the end button.

But no way was I giving up that easily.

I hopped in my roadster (fire engine red – if you're buying a car for show, might as well go all out, right?) and drove over the hill to the Waterston's address in Beverly Hills. It was a large, brick and white columned affair that spoke of someone's obsession with *Gone with the Wind*. Singularly out of place in sunny California. And crawling with press.

I parked my car down the block, scanning the line of reporters for any way to slip inside unnoticed. They were two and three deep near the driveway, a few even going so far as to set up camp on the Waterston's front lawn. I had a sinking feeling if there was any way to get in or out, Mrs. Waterston had already taken it.

I flipped open my glove box and pulled out a plastic laminated press pass. Or at least, a really good replica of a press pass that had served me well on more than one occasion. I looped the lanyard around my neck and hopped out, jogging over to the line of vultures waiting to prey on Mrs. Waterston's media carcass.

Near the front drive I spotted a guy wearing a windbreaker emblazoned with the Channel 4 logo.

"Hey, Bob, right?" I asked, coming up behind him.

He turned, giving me a view of his jowly cheeks and sprayed-in-place hair. "Chip."

"Right, sorry. Chip. I'm so bad with names. But I recognize you from Channel Four. You work with Soledad, right?" I asked, pulling out the name of the reporter I'd seen on TV last night

Chip gave me a quick up and down. "And you are?"

"Jamie Gonzales. Telemundo." I flashed my fake press pass.

"Right. Hi, how are you?"

"Great. Listen, our news van got caught in traffic, and we just got here. Any chance you could catch me up? Is the wife in there?"

Chip shrugged. "I think so. The only people in or out all day have been crime scene techs and plainclothes."

I looked toward the front door. A group of said plainclothes officers was huddled there now, their backs to the press as they bent their heads together.

"They come out with anything new this morning?" I fished.

"Not that they're sharing."

"Any comment from the family?"

Chip shook his head. "Sorry."

"Hmm. Well, thanks for the update."

I turned and was about to head back to my car, relieved at least Mrs. Waterston hadn't been seen being escorted out in handcuffs, when one of the plainclothes broke free from the rest, moving around the side of the house. He was dressed in a tailored grey suit, way beyond the financial confines of a cop's salary, and, as he moved around the corner, I got a glimpse of his face. Tanned skin, green eyes, blonde hair gelled into place.

I froze. I knew that face.

What the hell was Brooks Brothers doing here?

"Chip!" I barked.

"Yeah?"

I gestured to my admirer from the fundraiser as he crossed the lawn. "Who is that?"

Chip followed my line of vision. "Grey suit?"

I nodded, my gaze still pinned to the man.

Chip chuckled. "Lady, are you new or just been living under a rock the last six months?"

I clenched my jaw, tearing my eyes away from Brooks Brothers long enough to shoot Chip a look. "Humor me, okay? Do you know him?"

He grinned. "Yeah, I know him. He's Aiden Prince. The goddammed ADA."

CHAPTER FIVE

———

I blinked. My mental hamster momentarily stunned on his wheel as I starred at Chip. "ADA? As in Assistant District Attorney?"

He nodded. "That's the one."

Shit.

Not only had my client killed her husband based on the motive *I'd* provided her with, but turns out the guy in charge of prosecuting her wanted to sleep with me. Derek was going to have a field day with this one.

I halfheartedly thanked Chip and dug my cell from my pocket as I walked, head down, back to my car. Maya picked up on the first ring.

"The Bond Agency?"

"Emergency. I want you to get me everything you can on an Aiden Prince. ADA. Now!"

"Right. Two seconds." I heard her fingers flying over her keyboard. A beat later she fired back with, "Aiden Prince, 38, graduate of Yale Law, recently employed as an L.A. County Assistant District Attorney. Previously with the Kansas City district attorney's office, wife died last year from breast cancer, and he relocated to L.A. Oh, how sad."

"Anything else?"

"He's a leftie, ran in the L.A. marathon this year, and donated $20,000 to juvenile diabetes charities last fall. Give me ten minutes, and I can have his credit history."

"Don't bother. Thanks, Maya."

"Any time."

I hung up and slipped inside my roadster.

I tapped my fingernails on the console as I watched Aiden examine a spot on the ground. He knelt, careful not to put his knee in the wet soil, poked at something with a pen, then turned and gestured to a colleague – this one clearly marked as a cop by his Sears quality suit. The cop bent down, looked at the ground, then both men straightened and put their heads together, talking, serious expressions marking their brows.

I would have given my fav Louboutin's to know what they were saying.

Instead, I put my car in gear and pulled away from the curb, pointing it toward Studio City.

As soon as I hit my apartment, I grabbed the trashcan from my bedroom and dumped the contents on the floor, rummaging through until I laid hands on the cocktail napkin. I smoothed it out on my dresser, reached for the pre-paid cell I kept in my nightstand, and dialed the number before I could change my mind.

One of the things Derek taught me when reluctantly handing over the reins of the agency was to purchase an untraceable burner phone, saying it often "came in handy". This was one of the first times I was glad I had listened to him.

It rang. And again. Five rings into it, I was just about to give up when his voice picked up.

"Prince here."

"Hi, Aiden? It's Jamie."

Silence on the other end.

"We met the other night. At the fundraiser? Black dress?"

Still silent. Great. How many napkins had this guy given out?

"The tall blonde?" I prompted again.

"Right, right," he said, recognition dawning. "Hi. Sorry, it's been a long day."

Tell me about it.

"Anyway," I went on, "it was so nice meeting you. I... well, I honestly haven't been able to stop thinking about you."

"Really?" He didn't sound like he was entirely buying it. "And here I thought I'd struck out."

"Oh, no. You made quite an impression." Which, as of half an hour ago, was the truth.

"Well, I'm glad you called, Jamie. I'm pleasantly surprised."

"That's me. Full of surprises. So, how have you been?"

"Ah, good. Fine. Sorry, I'm, uh, just a little distracted at the moment."

"Work?"

"Yeah."

"What do you do, Aiden?"

"I'm a lawyer."

"What kind?"

"Criminal."

"Defense or prosecution."

"Prosecution."

"No kidding? Any chance you're working that case where the judge was shot?"

"It's a big case," he hedged.

"Talked to the wife yet?"

"You ask a lot of questions, Jamie."

I bit my lip. Too far?

"Just trying to get to know you, Aiden," I said, pouring on the charm.

"Apparently. Listen, I'm kind of tied up here. How about I give you my life story over drinks tonight?"

Not exactly how I'd envisioned this conversation going. But...

"Alright."

"Yeah? Great. Uh, say around nine?"

"Perfect."

"Okay. Great, okay then. Listen, I'm really sorry, but I've got to go. But I'll call you on this number later tonight, okay?"

"Looking forward to it, Aiden. Looking forward to it."

I hit the end button and dropped down on my bed.

Okay, so maybe no one was talking to the press. But there was a chance that "Jamie Smith" and her fuck-me heels might be able to garner a little more information out of our ADA than Chip and company. Like *if* the cops were looking at the wife, *if* she'd told them about our little sting operation, and *if* the Bond Agency was about to be plastered all over CNN as the purveyor of murder motives to unhappy housewives everywhere.

If I was lucky, I might even be able to persuade Aiden to keep the agency out of the investigation altogether.

As gears turned in my head, my cell rang.

"Hello?" I answered. In a voice that, in hindsight, might have been a little on the imagining-seducing-an-ADA-for-insider-info side.

"Wow. Sexy. Who did you think was calling? 'Cause I know that wasn't for me."

Danny.

"No one," I hedged.

"Uh-huh. So, you just answer the phone like a sex kitten all the time? Remind me to call you more often."

"I was not being a sex kitten."

"Trust me, you keep talking like that, and you can start charging three-ninety-nine a minute."

"Thanks for the tip," I mumbled, making a concerted effort to give my voice a pissed off edge. "And, by the way, where were you last night? I was two seconds away from a complete meltdown, and you wouldn't pick up your phone."

"I had company," he responded, and I could almost see the smirk on his face. "A couple of nice, young, redheaded bits of company with huge sets of..."

"Halt! No more details. I get the picture. I take it you were too busy to watch the news, then?"

"Never watch the news. Too depressing. Why? What happened? Brad and Angie splitting?"

"I wish. No, Judge Waterston."

"What about him?"

"He took a bullet to the head yesterday afternoon."

Danny was silent on the other end. Then, "Holy shit. What happened, James?"

I filled him in as best I could. Which, considering all I knew came from Soledad and Tom at the news desk, wasn't much.

When I was done, Danny just did a low whistle. "Wow. Sucks, babe."

"That seems to be the general consensus."

"But you know this isn't your fault. People do weird things. You can't predict them."

"I know." And I did. It just didn't make me feel any better.

"Hey, what are you doing right now?" he asked.

I looked down at the cocktail napkin. "Nothing."

"Cool. Want to meet for a late lunch?" he asked. "My treat."

I shrugged. Who was I to turn down a free meal?

* * *

Twenty minutes later I met Danny near his place in Santa Monica at the Dungeon, a pizza and hoagie joint with no windows, peeling paint and the absolute best pastrami and onion sandwiches in the known universe. A large, stained bar spanned one side of the room, with a handful of wooden table and chairs sets and a scarred pool table taking up the bulk of the tiny place. A TV was mounted on the ceiling in one corner, the guy behind the bar flipping between a soccer match and the news. Danny was waiting for me at the bar, already working his way through a Budweiser.

"Hey, kid," he said when he saw me approach. He looked down at my snakeskin pumps. "Nice shoes."

"Thanks."

"You fight a rattler for those?"

"Nope, just a pushy gay salesman. You order yet?"

"Two hot pastramis, coming right up."

"You are a god."

He grinned, flashing white teeth at me. "That's what the redheads said, too."

I rolled my eyes. "Spare me."

I perched on the stool next to him and signaled the bartender, a middle aged guy with pock marks and thick, bushy eyebrows that were barely independent of each other, for a beer of my own.

"So, how'd you and Sam do with Shankman?" I asked.

Danny shook his head. "No deal. Nanny did the laundry, then went to Starbucks. The mister spent his lunch hour on the phone in his den."

"Great."

"Buck up, kid. We'll try again tomorrow. I got a feeling he can't keep it in his pants for long."

"Let's hope," I mumbled. Because Mrs. Waterston's cash was only going to last us so long.

Five minutes later I was enjoying a cold Budweiser and a steamy plate of hot, thin sliced pastrami on a Kaiser with browned onions and lots of spicy mustard. It was as close to heaven as I could get with all of my clothes on. I heard Danny moan beside me, echoing my sentiments. We ate in silence, each of us completely engrossed in our gluttonous meals, only vaguely listening to the drone of the television behind us.

Until, once again, Soledad began talking about everyone's favorite deceased judge.

"Tom, we've just received some breaking news about the shooting death of Judge Thomas Waterston…"

I groaned. "See what I mean?" I asked around a melt-in-your-mouth bite. "This case is a media feeding frenzy. Clients are going to start dropping like flies."

Danny grinned. "Cheer up. You can always change your slogan. 'We track 'em down, you shoot 'em up.'"

I punched him in the arm. "Ha. Ha. Very funny."

"Ow." Danny rubbed his arm in mock pain. "You've been working on that right hook, haven't you?"

I ignored him, taking another mouthful of pastrami as Soledad shared her breaking news with the viewing public.

"Just moments ago we at Channel Four obtained exclusive video of a suspect police now believe may have played a role in the judge's death. Tom, police tell us they are looking for this woman."

I glanced up at the TV.

Then nearly choked on my hoagie as an image of myself in a slinky black dress filled the screen.

"Holy shit," I heard Danny mutter. But my entire being was focused on the words pouring out of Soledad's perfectly painted mouth.

"Police are looking for any information regarding the whereabouts of this woman, known only as 'Jamie Smith,'" she continued. "She was apparently the last person to see the judge alive, and, as you can clearly see here, she is instructing Judge Waterston to room three-eighteen, outside which, as you know, his body was ultimately found the following day."

Somehow I managed to swallow the bite of pastrami and onions that had turned to lead in my throat. He'd been found outside room three-eighteen? How could that be? I'd made it up; it was all lies. There was no one waiting for him in three-eighteen.

"Do they know yet how this person was connected to the judge?" Tom asked from off screen.

Soledad shook her bob back and forth. "No, Tom. The only information we have comes from this footage."

I stared at the screen, frozen as I watched myself tell the judge where to meet me, saw his pleased reaction, then his hand cupping my ass as I giggled flirtatiously.

I grabbed my Budweiser and took a long swig, wishing like hell it was something stronger. I thought I heard Danny talking beside me, something about calling a lawyer.

But honestly none of it sunk in. I closed my eyes, trying to keep my head from spinning right off my shoulders. Where the hell had the press gotten that footage? Had the judge really gone up to room three-eighteen? Had someone followed him? And what about his wife?

As if to answer my question, Soledad piped up from the corner again.

"Tom, we go live now to the judge's widow, Veronica Waterston, speaking out about these newest developments."

"Our family is doing its best to cope with this tragedy," came the widow's voice.

Only it wasn't her voice. She sounded like she'd smoked three packs a day for the last sixty years. And not the slightest hint of a Hepburn accent.

My eyes shot open. I stared at the TV screen mounted above the wooden bar as the image of a portly, grey-haired woman in dark polyester filled the screen. Below her ran a banner bearing the name "Veronica Waterston."

If this was the judge's wife, who the hell had come into my office?

Every fiber in my body froze in place, my swirling brain suddenly focusing with alarming clarity on just one terrifying thought.

I'd been set up.

CHAPTER SIX

———

Who?

The word, along with a colorful array of obscenities, looped through my mind. Who was the fake Mrs. Waterston? Who'd pretend to be the wife of a Superior Court judge? Who'd hire a private investigator to prove infidelity as a ruse?

A murderer looking for a scapegoat, that's who.

Who had been naive enough to take the word of a stranger at face value?

The answer sunk to the pit of my stomach and dueled with the pastrami.

Me.

When I looked up, the bartender averted his eyes. I whipped my head around, wondering how many other Dungeon patrons recognized the woman in the footage and the woman sitting at the bar.

I glanced again at the bartender. He was intent on the register now, eyes down, forehead wrinkled in concern. Were his fingers itching to dial 911 and leave a tip? Eventually someone would point me out to the cops. And then what?

Danny touched my hand, jolting me from my thoughts. "This will get straightened out." But the pinched look on his face screamed panic more than reassurance.

I nodded. "She killed the judge and set me up to cover her tracks," I said, working through my jumbled thoughts out loud. "But why? And if she's not really the wife, who is she? What does she have to do with the judge?"

"I know a guy. A lawyer. He defended that athlete accused of murdering his wife. You know the one." He rapped his knuckles on the bar, as if the motion would dislodge the name from his brain.

"And beyond why him and why her... why me?" I asked no one in particular. "Why frame me?"

"A good lawyer will sort through it all."

"I have a lawyer."

Danny sighed and shook his head at me. "Not Levine. You need a criminal attorney."

I shivered, practically break dancing on the bar stool at the phrase. I'd been known to bend the law on occasion, but I was no criminal. Besides, who could afford a high profile lawyer? There was no reason I couldn't figure this out before it got to that. "The footage is the key to finding out who did this," I decided, staring at the TV screen again as if it might replay.

Danny blew out a long breath. "Are you listening? Bond, this is serious."

I was listening. I'd heard every syllable he uttered, every nuance in his tone, every stab at my competence. He didn't think I could handle this.

I pushed my plate away, clanking it into my beer bottle. I couldn't continue eating. "Lawyers hire P.I.s, Danny. Not the other way around."

"So you're gonna hire yourself?" He raised his smartass eyebrows.

"No, I'm going on my date with the ADA." I tossed several bills on the bar and grabbed my bag.

Danny held up a hand, palm out. "Whoa. What are you talking about?"

I told him about my call with Aiden. When I was done, he looked at me like I needed committed.

"Are you crazy? You'll be wearing handcuffs before appetizers."

I rolled my eyes, knowing full well it made me look like a petulant teenager. I only dusted off the expression for him and Derek.

"I know what I'm doing. I'm not a rookie when it comes to men," I said, driving home the point that I didn't need an extra father. One was more than enough.

Another patron walked in as I stood and gave me the body check. My skin prickled. Maybe he was just checking out my hot pumps and short skirt... or maybe he'd seen Soledad's report and was even now counting the reward money in his head. Either way, the mingling aromas of old grease, stale beer and musty men funked my personal space. I couldn't sit there any longer.

"I need to get out of here," I said, leading the way to the parking lot.

"So the sex kitten voice was for the Ken doll," Danny said, following me.

Sunlight blinded me, and I reached into my bag for my Gucci sunglasses, using the motion to ignore Danny's statement.

"Obviously he knows you're the prime suspect in his case."

"You think, Sherlock?"

"Well, clearly you can't lead with your libido."

I scoffed. "Is that what you think I'm doing? God, Danny, I'm not *you*. I want to find out what he knows. Find the fake Mrs. Waterston and nail her ass before someone nails mine, got it? I have no interest in romance, trust me."

Danny sighed and used his fingers as a wide-toothed comb, making his hair stand on end. "I don't like it."

"You don't have to. I have my big girl panties on. I can take care of myself."

I expected him to make a crude comment about my undergarments. Instead he said, "Fine, but I'm going with you."

I chuckled, hoping it sounded playful, even though it was laced with annoyance. "I said I could handle it."

But he ignored me. "I'll wire you and wait outside. But you're not going alone. Aside from wanting you behind bars, he's a creep, probably sleeps with every woman he meets."

Well if that wasn't the horndog calling the flirt a himbo.

But, considering I wasn't 100% sure he wasn't right, I relented. "Fine. Wire me."

And since Danny hadn't drilled the ADA's reputation into the concrete far enough, he added, "You can't trust this guy."

No shit. But it was the best lead I had at the moment. I planned to slide up to ADA Prince and gently squeeze out the info I needed. By the time I was done, Prince would know a new definition of the word charming.

* * *

I still had hours before I needed to get ready and meet Prince, and the last thing I wanted to do was pace my apartment, possibly collide into Levine at the office again, or run the risk of being seen at the target range.

With all of my regular hangouts off limits, I chose the only other place that held sentiment.

The grass crunched beneath my pumps. Too many days without rain and temps over ninety left it yellow and pea green in spots. Even without my jacket, I wanted to melt into the ground. I'd left it in the car, along with my gun, because she didn't approve of weapons.

At least that's what Derek had told me years ago.

She used to frown and complain when he'd come home wearing his. Mom lived an honest life, filled with peace and kind words. When she disciplined me, she never raised her voice, even while grounding me for what felt like life. She and Derek couldn't have been more different.

I turned off the narrow dirt path and walked up two rows to the back corner of the cemetery. Propped against her headstone sat a bouquet of wild flowers. Her favorites. Their vibrant purple, yellow, and pink petals were still smooth and fresh. Someone delivered them recently.

I smiled at the idea of an old friend paying his or her respects, of someone visiting so she wasn't lonely. Perhaps that was a silly notion, but I needed to believe she was still listening when I shared my life, still laughing at my goofs, still frowning at my mistakes.

I placed a smaller bouquet of the same blooms beside the first set and sat down. Leaning against her tombstone, I shut my eyes and pressed out the world, traveling back to a time before Bond Agency, before DeLine Models, and before the car accident.

"Do you remember that Christmas we spent in New York because we wanted to see the city and experience snow? I was so young. We went ice skating at Rockefeller Center, and you kept falling."

She'd worn a yellow scarf, and every time she went down, the frayed ends blew up and landed on top of her head. It reminded me of Big Bird and made me giggle.

"At the hotel that night, you lied in bed, your legs smothered in towels of ice. Then the next day, despite the aches and bruises, we went back and you managed to not fall…as much."

I chuckled at the memory. "You taught me how to keep going, Mom. Thank you."

Years later, I wondered if she'd fallen on purpose, just to hear me laugh. She was like that.

After a few moments of silence, I opened my eyes and filled her in on the latest. I hesitated at the part where my face was plastered on the local news, but she'd want to know every detail, so I reluctantly told.

The greatest thing about Mom was she never judged me. When I wanted to pierce my septum in fifth grade, because a hot drummer in a punk band did the same, she said, "You'd look great with a loop. Just take care of it and you won't develop any infections. They're easy to heal with medication though. It'll only be swollen and filled with puss for a few days."

Needless to say, my septum remained un-pierced to this day.

"Danny's wrong," I told her. "A lawyer's not going to help me. I mean, I can't just turn myself in. That's crazy. Right?"

A breeze stirred the ends of my hair. The aroma of jasmine floated with it.

Mom's signature scent.

The left side of my brain reasoned it belonged to nearby flowers, but the daughter in me felt her presence.

"I knew you'd agree."

My purse began to ring out an unfamiliar tone. I dug inside and came out with the prepaid cell, checking the readout.

Prince.

My pulse raced, feeling like life had suddenly intruded on my sanctuary.

I glanced to Mom as if looking for her input, then answered. "Hello?"

"Jamie? It's Aiden."

"Hi," I said slowly. "I wasn't sure if you'd call back."

"Why's that?" His voice was steady and business-like. Some small part of me was almost impressed with his game of chicken. It was the same tone he'd used only hours ago when he'd thought I was just a hot blonde and not a murder suspect. There was no hint of deceit in it whatsoever. He was good, I'd give him that.

A fact that made the pit of anxiety grow to epic proportions in my stomach.

"Just figured you may be too busy," I answered, trying to match his casual sound.

"I'd never cancel on a beautiful woman. So is nine still okay?"

"Great." The word came out rushed and way too eager.

"Good. How about we meet at Franco's? Are you familiar?"

A rustic Italian restaurant off Melrose. I'd never been inside, but I heard the Roasted Vegetable Lasagna was to die for.

"Yes, I can't wait."

"Me too. See you tonight."

The line went dead. I sat there staring at the phone, wondering if he'd actually show up or have a police cruiser waiting to escort me to the local precinct.

But my gut said to take the chance. If there was any possibility of getting answers, it was through the ADA.

CHAPTER SEVEN

I'd arrived at Franco's fifteen minutes early. Enough time to scope out the place and find a prime position for observing without being noticed. At the moment, a large wooden column was doing the trick just nicely.

Wood beams lined the ceiling, and pillars flanked the foyer. The dinning area had white linen tablecloths and dim lighting. Very atmospheric. The small bar held only a few seats, the bulk of the room taken up with romantic tables for two. Vaguely I wondered if Aiden had picked the venue before or after he realized I was his prime suspect.

The bartender, a slim man with a wiry mustache, looked up frequently while mixing drinks. It had to be the strapless, red mini dress that accentuated my legs and cleavage. Of course, it could've been the way I hid, pressed to the column like a stripper.

I refused to believe it could be because he'd seen the latest broadcast displaying my face as a *person of interest* in the judge's murder. I mean, who paid attention to those new briefs anyway? My firm grip on denial allowed my heart to continue beating at a moderately normal level.

"Jamie, he just pulled up." Danny's voice registered clearly in my earpiece.

Attached to the bodice of my dress was a diamond brooch with a hidden camera disguised inside. Not what I'd normally wear on a date, but tonight was all business.

"Copy that," I spoke into my chest, with a sigh of relief that he'd shown up himself.

And not sent a gang of black and whites.

The bartender frowned, probably wondering why the crazy, hot woman was talking to herself.

I offered a killer, um, no, an innocent smile and turned back to watch the entrance.

The door opened and Aiden strode in. He still wore the suit trousers he had on earlier, but the jacket and tie were removed, leaving the white button-down open just enough to catch a glimpse of his tanned chest.

He glanced toward the bar, and my palms began to sweat like a thirteen-year-old on her first date.

Jitteriness wasn't usually a part of the routine. But nothing was usual about this encounter.

The Maitre d' showed him to a table in the far, front corner.

From what I could tell there were no police cars out front, no flashing lights or sirens. He hadn't walked in with any officers, and he was reading the menu.

I turned my back to the bar and asked Danny, "How's it look out there?"

"All clear."

A hand clamped down on my shoulder, and I flinched. I spun around to find the Maitre d'—a stout man with white hair and skin as smooth as a helium-filled balloon.

"Madame, may I help you?" he asked, clearly not used to women hiding out in his restaurant.

So much for being incognito.

"I'm fine," I whispered. "I was set up on a blind date, and I wanted to scope him out first. You know."

But from the sudden creases along his forehead, he didn't. "Shall I show you to a table so you can wait for the gentleman?"

Danny chuckled in my ear. "Smooth, Jamie."

An older couple walked inside and stopped at the host stand.

Perfect timing.

I used their presence as a shield and stepped forward. "No need. I see him now."

The Maitre d' shot me a look that said he'd be keeping an eye on me (join the club, pal), but thankfully left me to attend to the new couple.

I took a deep breath. It was now or never.

Aiden looked up as I approached. His brows raised, and a smile tugged at his mouth. He stood and pulled out my chair.

"Play it cool," Danny whispered.

Like there was any other way?

"I'm so glad you called." Aiden widened his smile. The corners around his eyes creased. Under different circumstances, the expression would've been endearing. Right now, I wondered how he'd play his cards. I knew why I was here. Why was he?

"I'm glad your busy schedule allowed."

Danny scoffed.

As Aiden helped push in my chair, he received a wide angle view of my cleavage. Luckily I'd tucked the mic far enough down to be out of sight. There was no sense in wearing something this revealing if I wasn't going to flaunt it.

He returned to his seat. "I hope this is acceptable. I figured in case you're hungry. It's been a long day, and I'm famished."

He planned to feast on stuffed shells or Veal Piccata while interrogating me?

"Your job must be so demanding."

"There's that sex kitten voice again," Danny muttered under his breath.

I cleared my throat and watched Aiden from beneath my lashes.

"It has its moments," he answered. "And what about you? What does Jamie *Smith* do?"

Was he aware that he'd emphasized my fictitious last name? Was it on purpose? Was he trying to crack me, get a confession right here in the dim candlelight of our table for two?

I parted my lips, tempted to falsify my life with tales of yacht sailing and actual Prince ogling, when the waiter arrived with a glass of Chardonnay for Aiden and a martini for me.

"I hope you don't mind I ordered just before you arrived," Aiden explained.

"You remembered what I was drinking the other night." His attention to detail was, once again, annoyingly endearing.

And a bad sign of the thoroughness with which he did his job.

"Of course." He flashed a brilliant smile that probably made other women weak at the knees. Good thing I was seated.

The waiter asked, "Are you ready to order?"

"Give us a few, please." Aiden lifted his glass. He waited for the young man to walk off before saying, "Here's to getting to know one another."

I wrapped my hand around the stem of my glass, allowing the cone-shaped bowl to rest against the side of my palm. A slightly awkward grip, but it was better than leaving my prints on the glass.

His gaze traveled to my glass, aware of my avoidance. Or maybe I was reading too much into his gaze.

"So tell me about being a criminal attorney," I asked. "It must be immensely satisfying to lock away the bad guys."

He chuckled warmly. I had to admit, it was kind of a nice sound. "Yes, very."

"But it can't be easy. The burden of proof lies with the ADA, right?"

When he raised his brows, I added, "I watched a lot of *Law & Order*."

"Hollywood is fiction."

"True. So clue me in on the way it actually works." I sipped my drink. The vodka hit my belly and spread throughout my limbs. Now this was a drink.

He leaned back in his chair, never looking away. His posture conveyed confidence. His slicked-back hair conveyed confidence. His smirk conveyed confidence.

God, I wish I had some of that right now.

"What do you want to know?" he asked.

I gently set down the glass and eased into a similar position. "What about the case you mentioned? That judge."

"The one from the Hilton, where we met."

I kept my expression steady as we stared one another down, as if whoever blinked first would qualify as the loser. Luckily this was my favorite sport as a child. I'd never met a person I couldn't outstare, especially boys.

"Judge Waterston's killer shouldn't be too difficult to apprehend," he said slowly, blinking first.

"Oh, why's that? Did he leave behind a big clue?"

"You can say that."

I almost laughed out loud. Did he think his cockiness was going to make me confess?

"Be careful, James," Danny whispered into my ear.

My friend knew me too well, knew I wanted to prove how very wrong the ADA's assumptions were, but I continued with my stoic-slash-come-hither game face.

"I'd love to hear about it," I goaded.

"I'm sorry, I can't comment on an open investigation." He punctuated the statement with a wink, as if chalking up one point on his side of the scoreboard.

Fine. I had all night to dance around the judge. And the more sips of his chardonnay he took in the meantime, the easier it would be for me to lead.

"So, what brought you to the benefit the other night?" I asked, smiling sweetly his way.

"It's a cause I believe in strongly."

"Oh?"

He nodded, and for a half a second the confidence in his eyes gave way to something else. "Yes. Someone close to me died of breast cancer last year."

Oh hell. Had the benefit been a cancer awareness thing? I'd honestly never even paid attention.

"I'm sorry," I said, meaning it as I remembered what Maya had told me about his wife. Bringing up a personal death was a dirty trick. One I almost wanted him to know I hadn't played on purpose.

He looked down into his glass, swirling the few remaining inches in a circle to avoid looking at me. "It's fine. You didn't know."

I cringed.

"It's always hard to lose someone," I said. Which sounded like a hollow Hallmark sentiment even to my ears.

"It was my wife," he said, still not looking up.

Why he was telling me, I didn't know. Maybe some irrational need to open up. Maybe a ploy to get me to open up to him?

I feigned surprise and laid a hand on my chest, careful to avoid the camera. "That's horrible."

"It was, but we move on," he said, pasting a smile on his face that said he was doing just that with this conversation. "What about you? Have you ever been married?"

"God, no."

"And I'll assume, since we're sitting here, that you're not involved?"

"I'm single," I assured him.

"Good to know."

"I bet," Danny whispered.

"What do you do for fun, Jamie? How do you spend your nights?"

Was this his round-about way of asking for my alibi when the judge was murdered?

"I'm a people watcher," I replied honestly.

Danny snorted in my ear.

"I hang out with friends, have a few drinks, get a bite. The usual," I clarified.

"Do you have family in the area?"

I filed the thought of Derek into a locked safe and forgot the combination. "We're not close."

"What did you do after the benefit?"

Ah, direct. I glanced to my martini, wishing to down it in one gulp. I refrained however. "I went home. Straight to bed."

He smirked. "Let me guess. Red silk sheets?"

Danny continued his pig sounds.

I laughed, not expecting the question. "Six-hundred thread count Egyptian cotton."

"Nothing less than the best."

"Well, I have my eye on a set of fifteen-hundred count, but a girl's gotta eat. Is this where I ask, boxers or briefs?"

He chuckled in response. "Only if I get to ask the same."

Then he winked, and I couldn't help picturing his toned, tanned body above a pair of Calvin Kleins. It wasn't an unpleasant image.

"So, were you alone?" His smile was playful, but I was an expert at reading between the lines. *Do you have an alibi?*

"Oh, Aiden, a girl has to have some secrets." My turn to give the seductive wink. Score one for Jamie's side.

"Hmm." he said, sitting back in his chair.

But before he could pursue that thought, the server arrived to take our order. Aiden went with an appetizer of calamari. Even though the last thing that had touched my lips was the pastrami sandwich with Danny, food was light years from my mind. But, considering I was quickly draining my martini, I ordered a plate of bruschetta anyway. As soon as the man walked away, I turned my attention back to my prey.

"So, my turn to pry," I said, shooting Aiden my best flirtatious smile as I leaned my elbows on the table. "The judge that was killed. Did you know him?"

Aiden cocked his head to the side. "Why do you ask?"

I shrugged. "You both run in judicial circles. I thought maybe you've bumped into each other before at social events. Maybe he and his wife?"

Aiden paused, eyes scrutinizing me, wondering, I could tell, how much to give up. "I'd met him once or twice."

"What was he like?"

"Judicial."

"And his wife?"

"Sorry, we weren't that close," he said, cutting off that line of questioning.

"I saw something on the news," I said, flirting with dangerous territory. "Something about video footage from the night the judge died?"

"Careful, Bond," I heard Danny whisper in my ear.

While I appreciated the concern, careful was getting me nowhere. I was on borrowed time, I knew. How long before Aiden tired of the flirtation-slash-interrogation game and pulled out the handcuffs?

I watched him carefully as he answered. "Yes. I saw that, too."

"So, it's true? You have video of the judge from that night?"

"We do."

"Where did it come from?"

"Bond..." Danny warned in my ear. "You're treading on thin ice."

But I ignored him, watching the muscles in Aiden's jaw move as he decided just how to answer that question.

"Where it came from isn't as important as what's on it," he said.

"Huh," I answered, sitting back in my seat. "Odd."

"What's odd?" Aiden asked, taking my bait.

"Well, it's just that..." I paused, giving him my most innocent smile. "On *Law & Order* they always considered the source of the evidence as the main factor in how valid it was."

Aiden sat back, giving me a perfect poker face. "Are you saying the footage we have may be faked?"

I shrugged. "I'm saying things aren't always what they appear to be."

He gave me a long look that was completely unreadable. Then just when the silence was starting to make me sweat, said, "Channel Four."

"Excuse me?"

"The footage was sent to a local news station. Channel Four. They forwarded it on to us just before it aired."

Bingo.

I opened my mouth to respond, but before I had the chance, Danny piped up in my ear again.

"I got bad news, Bond," he shouted. "A couple of squad cars just pulled up. You need to get out of there. Now!"

CHAPTER EIGHT

———

I froze. It was all I could do to keep the smile pasted on my face as my body launched into fight or flight mode. Mostly flight.

"I need to use the restroom," I said, forcing myself to rise slowly from the table, despite instant panic urging me on. "Excuse me."

"I'll meet you at the side," Danny said, his voice mirroring my panic.

My hip knocked into the table, jostling the dinnerware. A butter knife slid off, and I caught it midway to the floor. I tossed it beside the bread plate and half-walked, half-sprinted to the foyer.

Once around the corner, I dropped the walking bit and just sprinted to the restrooms.

I would've preferred using the delivery doors, but accessing the kitchen from the dining room would've made Aiden suspicious. So I settled for Plan B. The ladies' room window. Danny and I had cased all outside exits before he dropped me off. This one was our best bet.

I tugged on the restroom door handle. It didn't budge. Shit. Occupied.

I glanced to a second door beside the restroom. The men's room. I hadn't actually checked it out, but it stood to reason there was a window in there, too. But as I reached for the handle, the Maitre 'd appeared in the hallway, wearing a scowl.

"May I help you?"

"No, thank you."

He stood firm, his grimace unwavering.

"I need to use the restroom," I whispered. I didn't need to fake the urgency in my voice.

"That is the men's room, Madame."

A scream, somewhere deep in my core, spiraled toward my throat. I was running out of time. It was all I could do to not push the old guy aside.

"I'm aware, but I really need to go."

I glanced at the front doors, expecting to see two uniformed officers with their guns aimed at my pretty head. It was clear but wouldn't be for long.

I grabbed the handle and pushed, but the door didn't budge. Occupied.

Something inside me fell, passed my other organs and landed at my Achilles heel. If I did the potty dance, could I convince this guy to let me use a back bathroom?

Unlikely.

Just then a stout woman in a royal blue, chiffon dress stepped out of the ladies' room.

A huge sigh escaped my mouth, and I almost threw my arms around her in a fierce hug. Instead I tossed a smirk over my shoulder to the Maitre d' and hurried inside.

I choked on a cloud of cheap perfume and breathed through my mouth. Not bothering to latch the door, I ran to the window. The frosted glass pane lifted with ease, and I used the trash can to hoist myself up.

Danny's van idled in the alley. He leaned out the driver's side window. "Hurry."

As if I was moving slow on purpose.

Legs over the ledge, I shimmied my torso forward. My dress caught on the sill, but I didn't care, didn't want to take the time to gingerly untangle the fabric, didn't want to add silver handcuffs to my accessories. I jumped and only hoped the ripping sound wouldn't leave my ass exposed.

As my feet touched the asphalt, one heel snapped, and I fell onto hands and knees. Scraped and bloodied, I hopped up with the grace of a drunken alley cat.

I waddled around the front of the van, temporarily blinded by the headlights, and scrambled into the passenger seat.

"That was close." Danny spun the vehicle away from the restaurant, turning left at the end of the alley.

To my right, I could see red and blue lights flashing against the front signage of the restaurant. I felt that panic slowly melting into relief as I pictured the look on Aiden's mouth, when he realized I'd escaped.

* * *

I paced the length of my desk, back and forth, grinding my heels into the carpet and my molars into enamel dust. Staying here, cooped up, while the girls were out talking to our source at Channel Four made me want to shred off the vanilla striped wallpaper with my fingernails.

Since I was too much of a control freak to relax and wait, Danny hooked the girls up. Microphones, cameras, the usual, but this time he managed to stream the feed, from Caleigh's chest to my laptop. Any minute now I'd be able to watch.

From the sidelines.

This was the first time I hadn't taken lead on a case so important.

Maya knocked on my door and entered. "Here. I thought you could use this." She handed me my usual—a grande, nonfat Caramel Macchiato.

She eyed the indentations my heels made in the carpet. "Maybe you don't need the caffeine."

"Thanks," I muttered and took a long, scalding sip.

Then to Danny, on speakerphone, I asked, "How's it going there?"

As if on cue, the black screen on my laptop grew static then flickered in and out.

"You got a picture?" Danny asked.

I made out double glass doors with the Channel Four logo. Maya and I moved closer.

"It's kinda fuzzy."

"Hey, it's the best I can do on short notice, kid," Danny replied.

I watched Sam and Caleigh walk into the lobby. I cranked up the volume on my speakers and sat in my chair. Maya pulled an imitation leather one over, and we huddled by the screen.

Our view sashayed across the burgundy carpet. Except for a young girl watering a nearby plant, the room appeared empty.

"Hey. I'm looking for Elaine," Caleigh said in her sweet as molasses drawl.

The girl turned, displaying a top row of barely detectable Invisalign braces and a set of double Ds that would put Dolly Parton to shame. She had light brown hair, feathered at the sides, channeling the original *Charlie's Angels,* and large green eyes. She wore a tank top that barely contained her non-bouncing boobs—clearly the work of a talented plastic surgeon.

"I'm her. Who are you?" Her smile appeared innocent, but her smoked-a-pack-a-day voice shattered that image.

"Whoa. Way to ruin a hottie." Danny's shock traveled across the phone line.

The girls must've felt the same way because it took Caleigh a moment to respond. "Hi, we're friends of Derek. He said you could help us."

Elaine set down the watering can and took a seat behind the long, counter-height front desk. It practically swallowed her whole.

"So what can I do Derek for?" She cackled.

I envisioned him and this child-like woman on his bed, in positions a daughter should never imagine. I shuddered.

Sam leaned down and rested her arms on the top edge of the desk. Her dark curls bounced into view. "The station received a package. A video of Judge Waterston on the night he was killed. We're hoping you can tell us about it. Like who sent it."

Elaine pursed her lips. "I wasn't here when it arrived. I didn't see who delivered it."

"Maybe someone else did?" Caleigh prodded.

"Or you can show us the envelope it arrived in," Sam suggested.

Elaine leaned back. "Why would I do that?"

"Derek said you were ever so helpful." Caleigh added extra syrup to her words.

Static buzzed in and out, and the picture skipped a beat. I prayed the feed would stay up. I trusted the girls. They were the best at what they did, but since this morning, I'd been a mass of anxiety. A rough night of tossing, turning, and thinking had me frazzled.

"Aww, Derek's just the sweetest man I've ever known," Double D purred.

Derek Bond? As in the man who shared half my DNA?

She leaned closer. "And the dirtiest old kook."

Ah, yes. That sounded about right.

"He once tied me up and slathered..."

I grabbed my ears, pressing my palms against my head with enough force to pop the top off a stubborn pickle jar, and held on for dear sanity. "La-la-la-la-la."

Maya smirked and kept her gaze on the screen. A moment later, she gave me the thumbs up, and I cautiously lowered my hands.

"Wait here," Elaine said then sprung out of her chair and hurried down a narrow corridor to a back office.

Static interfered, and when it cleared up, Elaine flounced back into view. She carried a pink, blue and yellow striped envelope.

The video arrived in that?

"I really shouldn't show you this, but I'd do anything for Derek." Another cackle set the hairs on my arms erect. "I pulled it from the trash for you."

Caleigh took the envelope and held it at an angle for the camera. Other than the postage corner and address label, it was devoid of any identifying marks.

"Damn." I punched the top of my desk. A cup of pens rattled. Maya flinched.

"It was a long shot," Danny said.

I rolled my eyes, wanting to hang up on him. I knew that, but it didn't mean I couldn't set my expectations high.

"It obviously came from a woman," Elaine chuckled. "Unless some man likes pink stripes and designer envelopes."

Designer. That was it.

"Danny, tell Caleigh to flip it over and look for a brand."

Maya scooted closer to my laptop. "What are you thinking?"

"You can't buy those at the post office. If she had them custom-made or even used a credit card, maybe we can find her identity."

Caleigh flipped the package and held the bottom left corner closer to her bosom.

Advent Paper.

The phone in the reception area rang. Maya scrambled up front, and I sat back in my chair, proud of our accomplishment. I watched Caleigh and Sam thank Elaine, who asked them to tell Derek she'd be calling soon for another wild ride. Gag. Then the reception went to permanent static, and Danny signed off.

"We're on our way."

Before I got a second to instruct Maya to search the name, my office door opened again. This time Levine stuck his head in.

He pointed behind him. "Maya was busy, so I let myself in."

Fab. Just what my day needed. A lecture on either a) criminal defense or b) firing an employee.

He lowered himself into the chair Maya had occupied, folding one leg over the other. "So I heard about your narrow escape last night."

"From whom?" The girls knew better than that. If one of them had talked to Levine, I might reconsider the firing thing.

"Danny mentioned it," he said.

Traitor.

"So, was it worth it?" Levine asked me, a hint of sarcasm in his voice.

"Yes, absolutely," I answered with confidence that I didn't quite yet feel. "We're following up a lead right now."

He narrowed his beady eyes, twitched his nose. I almost offered him the chunk of Munster in the back of the office fridge. Instead, I filled him in on the package.

When I finished, he finally said, "I'll set up an appointment with Mr. Prince, and we'll tell your side of the story."

Were brain cells leaking through his bald spot?

"So then he can have police and handcuffs waiting? I don't think so."

"Jamie, we can settle this with one meeting."

"How? Do you possess a magic wand I don't know about? My face is on that video."

"They only want you in for questioning. There's no proof to tie you to the murder, no DNA or fingerprints." He paused. "Right?"

Did he doubt me?

"Of course not, but I'm not taking that chance. We'll track down this package and find Faux Mrs. Waterston. Then we'll take *her* on a visit to the ADA."

He shook his head. "As your attorney, I don't agree. But, you're the client. I can't force you to do anything you don't want to."

Damned straight.

"So, you want to ignore the colossal legal mistakes you're making? Fine. Let's talk business instead. Which girl are you letting go?"

"Ha." I rose and walked to the door, signaling the end of this conversation. "I still have over a week to get us into the black."

"You're kidding me, right?" He stood and walked to me. "You're a suspect in a murder, Jamie."

"I'm aware."

"If your true identity leaks, this agency may as well hang up its shingle."

I straightened his tie. "They're letters painted on glass. Not a shingle."

The left corner of his mouth lifted. "You're just like your father."

I gently swatted his arm. "Of all the insults."

"Same determination. Same stubborn-streak." With that bit of indigestion, he turned and walked out. "We'll talk tomorrow."

Not if I solved this today.

I watched Levine leave, nearly colliding with Caleigh as she walked in with a proud smile. Danny followed a step behind.

"Where's Sam?" I asked.

"On the way back, she got a call from her sitter. Something about a stomachache, so she went home."

Watching Samantha load and shoot a gun like Rambo sometimes made me forget her other job was titled "Mom".

"Hope her kid's okay," I said.

Maya struck the keys on her keyboard with her French-manicured acrylic tips. "So I found Advent Paper's website. As it turns out, they're an online store that specializes in envelopes, stationary, parchment. Who knew there were so many paper choices?"

Caleigh walked around the reception desk and stared at the screen. She tapped Maya's shoulder with the back of her hand. "Let me at it."

Maya stood and gave up her seat.

"It shouldn't be too hard to get into their database and find their customer list."

While she attacked the keys, Danny grabbed my elbow and pulled me out of their earshot. "I saw Levine drive off as we pulled in."

"Yeah. Thanks for ratting me out, by the way."

At least Danny had the decency to look sheepish. "He called me last night after I got home. He said he wanted to help you."

"Yeah, well, he's delusional. He thinks talking to the ADA will be enough to clear me."

Danny paused, chewing on that thought. "I can't say I totally agree with that strategy. That Prince guy was shifty last night. I don't trust him."

"That makes two of us," I mumbled.

"But, Levine is a good lawyer. If he says you should turn yourself in..."

I stared at him as he trailed off. "Really? Et tu, Danny?"

"Got it," Caleigh cried, saving him from answering.

Damn, that girl was fast. We hurried to the desk. She clicked the mouse, and the printer hummed to life.

"There are five customers who purchased this paper in the past year."

"Not a big seller," I mumbled.

Caleigh walked to the end of the desk and lifted the page from the printer's tray. "Crystal McKinley," she said, reading the first name from the list.

Maya slid back into her chair.

I circled the desk as she brought up Google. Links to a Crystal McKinley's *Facebook* and *Tumblr* appeared at the top of the page. Maya clicked the *Facebook* link, and we were taken to a page of a teenaged redhead sporting a duck-face and inch-thick black eyeliner under her eyes.

"They really should offer cosmetology classes in high school," Caleigh said.

"That's definitely not her," I said.

"Okay, how about Edgar Washington."

Maya's fingers flew across the keys as Caleigh spoke, so by the time I could remind them we weren't looking for a man, an image of a wrinkled guy with skin the color of ash sprang up.

"Pass."

"Well, I guess we can also cross off Timothy Weiner. That's leaves Donna Martinez and Gail Baxter."

Maya clicked a few more keys, typing in the names. A moment later a picture of Faux Mrs. Waterston filled the monitor. Instead of the Audrey Hepburn look though, she wore her long, dark hair down. It flowed over her shoulders and she appeared softer, more angelic than the woman I'd met.

A flood of anger hit me.

She definitely had a talent for disguise. If she wasn't a murderer or trying to frame me, she'd make a great Bond girl.

"That's her."

Donna Martinez.

CHAPTER NINE

———

"Donna Martinez lists her profession as actress," Maya informed us, clicking open another window. "But, according to the IMDB, she hasn't had any significant roles. Not even a commercial."

IMDB was the Internet Movie Database, and if Donna had done anything from extra work in an indie flick to voice-over in a cartoon, it would have been there. "Wanna-be," I concluded, not surprised as the title covered half the residents of the L.A. Basin. "So what does she really do?

"Works nights as a cocktail waitress at Club Dante," said Maya, switching to another screen. "If her electronic fund transfers are any indication."

"I know that place. It's off Sunset," Caleigh jumped in. "It's nice. Swanky. I saw a Kardashian there last month."

"She's married to Miguel Martinez," Maya continued.

"Why does his name sound familiar?" Danny asked.

Maya clicked away at the keyboard, pulling up another window. "Miguel Martinez was arrested and sent to prison for aggravated assault last summer. He held up a liquor store and beat the clerk, who needed twenty stitches and suffered a concussion."

"I remember that story," Danny said, nodding as recognition dawned. "Double-jointed Brandy talked about it non-stop one night. She lived around the corner from the store."

Fascinating stuff, Danny.

"Miguel's no longer in prison. He died... oh."

"Oh?" I asked, leaning forward to read the screen.

"He died just last month. Stabbed by another inmate," Maya said.

Danny moved his head up and down with slow, deliberate nods, a stupid grin plastered on his face. "Shanked."

Caleigh, peering over Maya's shoulder, tapped the screen with a fingernail. "He was sentenced by Judge Waterston."

Damn. Talk about motive for revenge. The excitement buzzed through me, like a fluorescent light flickering to life.

Danny and I exchanged ah-ha glances. "I'll get the van," he said and hurried outside.

"Maya, jot down her address." I ran to my office and strapped on my holster and gun. I shrugged into my jacket, and slid my phone into a pocket.

When I turned, Caleigh leaned in the doorframe.

"Are you sure it's okay to go out there? What about the police?"

Her concern made me smile. "I'll be fine. If the cops knew about Donna, they'd also have the killer and no longer need me for anything. When I get back, this will be all over, and we can concentrate on our other clients."

I squeezed her shoulder and walked back into the lobby.

Maya handed me a sticky note with an address on it and wished us luck.

In the van, I gave Danny the lime green square with the addy and fastened my seatbelt. The ride along the freeway felt like hours, even though we'd hit a rare traffic-free sweet spot. I jiggled my knee up and down, too much adrenaline making it impossible to sit still.

Danny glanced over. "Antsy?"

I tried to chuckle, but it was a strangled sort of sound instead. "What gave me away?" I joked.

His tight smile did nothing to reassure me. Levine might be delusional, but Danny knew as well as I did how deep in dog crap I was. It wasn't a situation I was used to or, quite honestly, knew what to do with. Private investigators tracked down others. They didn't become the prey.

We pulled up outside of a squat, stucco building in North Hollywood with paint that was faded to a pale sun-stroked beige. It reminded me of a motel; two-stories tall, entrances facing the street. The building was divided in half, each with its own staircase weaving up the floors.

The apartment number on the Post-It was 2B, which I spotted immediately. The front window's curtains were parted, but with the sun's glare, I couldn't see any movement inside.

So we sat and watched.

I texted Maya for information on the type of car Donna drove, wishing I'd seen Faux Mrs. Waterston arrive and leave the agency. I mentally noted a beat-up green Hyundai, shiny, white Buick and muddy, black Trailblazer parked across from us now.

"This whole thing will be cleared up by tonight," Danny said.

I exhaled, grabbing onto his words with both hands. "I can't wait. My celebration will consist of a strong drink and a hot bubble bath." I imagined sinking into the fragrant soapy goodness.

"Alone? Or will you invite Mr. ADA?"

I jerked my head toward him. "What?"

"Just wondering. You two seemed pretty cozy last night."

I frowned. "You have to be joking. That was a cat and mouse game. I was flirting to save my life, Danny."

"Are you sure?"

An image of Aiden's cool eyes and warm smile flooded my vision. I quickly snuffed it out.

"Positive," I said. But my voice cracked.

Danny's eyebrows rose. "Not convincing, Bond."

"Jesus, would you drop it, Danny? Fine - Aiden Prince is an attractive man. Is that what you want me to say?"

He turned his gaze out the window, his expression hidden. "No. It's not."

I poked him in the arm. "Don't tell me you're jealous?" I teased.

He let out a sharp bark of laughter. "Of what? Slick hair and a spray-on tan?" He patted his abdomen. "A six-pack beats that any day."

I snorted. "You think pretty highly of yourself there, Casanova."

"Hey, I've never gotten any complaints."

I held up my hands. "I wasn't putting you down. Lord knows you've had every bimbo from here to Manhattan fall at your feet."

He turned on me. "Is that it? Just because I get laid that somehow puts me in a different league than Mr. Ken Doll?"

"What league, Danny?" I asked. "I said he was attractive, that's all."

"Yeah, he's a real catch, with is flashy career, making peanuts working for the state, and his dead wife sympathy card."

I stared at him, stunned into silence.

He paused a moment, then averted his gaze, as if realizing how far below the belt that comment had struck. "I don't trust him, that's all," he mumbled.

"That makes two of us."

We didn't say anything more, just sat there watching 2B.

Maya texted back that Donna Martinez had a valid California state driver license, but there was no info on the type of car she drove. Same went for her late husband.

Several tenants in surrounding apartments came and went, but there was no activity at Donna's. After another thirty, butt-numbing minutes, I decided we'd waited enough.

I grabbed the door handle. "Let's go have a look."

We exited the van and sprinted across the street. Early Friday afternoon meant most people were at work. Would that include wanna-be-actresses?

I knocked on her door, praying no one would answer. As much as I wanted to haul her ass to the local precinct, I also wanted to find proof of her involvement in setting me up and murdering the judge. A handwritten document detailing her plan to frame me and kill the judge would be a bit much to ask for, but a girl could hope.

When no one came to the door, I pulled a pouch of tools from my jacket pocket, ready to put my lock picking skills to work.

But before I even opened the little black case, Danny turned the knob and pushed. The door creaked open.

"Who doesn't lock their door in North Hollywood?" he whispered.

Agreed. This was not a good sign.

We slowly stepped over the threshold, and I called out. "Mrs. Martinez? Anyone home?"

Was it possible she'd seen us coming and hid? If so, I planned to go through every square inch. If she was quivering in a closet, we'd find her.

Daylight streamed through the window, illuminating a small, pastel living area. A light blue sofa took up most of one wall. A white coffee table sat in the center of the beige carpet. A television, a couple of cheap end tables, a short bookcase, and a lemon-colored chair completed the tidy set up. The place looked like a photo shoot for Pottery Barn and smelled of cinnamon and vanilla. All very feminine.

A thin stack of mail sat on a side table. An electric bill, flyer for 20% off at Macy's One Day sale and the latest copy of Cosmo were all addressed to Donna Martinez. At least we had the right apartment.

Sadly, no murder weapons, no confessions, and no Donna.

"Look." Danny pointed to a sheet of paper sitting on the coffee table. It had the same print as the striped envelope.

I walked over and scanned it.

Dear Mr. Sterling,

Thank you for your consideration in the role of Jacqueline Bouvier Kennedy Onassis. She was such a classic beauty and magnificent woman. I am so honored to have been given the opportunity.

Sincerely,

Donna Martinez

I raised a brow and glanced at Danny. "Is she serious? What decade is she from? Who sends thank you notes to casting directors?"

Danny chuckled. "Maybe she thinks this will raise her chances."

"Yeah, of being laughed at." I returned the absurd letter to the table, beside a pack of matches and an empty envelope with a scribbled phone number. I pulled out my phone and entered the digits into my contact list for future inquiry. Then I wandered into the back hall.

Three doors stood ajar. I poked my head into the first room. The kitchen counters and spotless stove stated Donna was either a clean freak or a take-out connoisseur. No desire to witness her OCD array of cans and boxes in the cabinets, I turned to the next room.

I ignored the pristine bathroom, figuring I'd raid the medicine cabinet last, and entered her bedroom. The place were secrets where hidden.

Holy fashion explosion.

If the rest of the house was considered tidy, this room resembled the regurgitated remains of a bargain basement sale. The sheets on the Queen-sized bed were rumpled. A pink and white polka dot comforter was tossed in a heap on the floor. Clothing covered every surface, including the lamp shade and window sill.

On my way to the open closet, I slipped on a grey graphic tee, and grabbed onto the door to prevent falling. Dresses, skirts, blouses and sweaters were neatly hung on half the rod. The other half was empty.

I paused. Took a good look at the clothing on the floor.

The room was covered in t-shirts, jeans... men's clothes.

Miguel's things.

I ransacked the top shelf of shoe boxes to find one stuffed with old photos of Donna and people I assumed were family and friends, and a wedding picture of her and Miguel. Crumpled receipts, dated as far back as three years ago, occupied another and a third held old letters from Miguel to Donna over the time he spent in prison.

I raised an eyebrow. Those held promise. Miguel could well have hatched the plan to kill the judge from behind bars. Maybe the letters contained explicit instructions on how to hire a sucker.

"Any luck in here?" Danny asked as he entered the room. Then paused. "Wow, tell me you didn't do this."

"Nope. This is all Donna. I haven't combed through the dresser yet."

Danny nodded, crossing to the pastel pink piece of furniture.

I sat on the edge of the bed, with the box in my lap and opened the first envelope. The letter was dated four months ago. He wrote that his cellmate was cool, but he missed her like hell, and it was unfair he was locked up.

There was a letter for each week of his incarceration. While his love for her never wavered, his attitude about everything and everyone else did. Over time, he ended up hating his cellmate but grew remorseful over the robbery. Unfortunately, there was no mention of Judge Waterston.

I returned the box to the closet. "Find anything useful?"

Danny turned. A pair of fuzzy, pink leopard handcuffs hung from his pinky finger. "Do these count?"

"Nice. Pure class."

"Wanna take the bathroom?" Danny asked.

I nodded, leaving him to explore the rest of Donna's goody drawer.

The white tiles gleamed. Frosted glass doors encased the tub, closed now, and a pair of towels hung over its rack. Two toothbrushes, one blue and one pink, leaned in a daisy ceramic cup. Tylenol, a dozen facial cleansers, moisturizers and acne medication stood at attention in the mirrored cabinet. The one beneath the sink held extra rolls of toilet paper, sanitary products and condoms. She had no prescriptions, nothing that told me anything personal.

Everything about Donna's apartment seemed staged, like she lived one giant role from sun up to sun down. This trip was starting to feel like a waste of time.

I turned to head into the kitchen, on the flimsy hope that her cabinets held the blueprint to framing Jamie Bond.

But a flash of something dark through the frosted bathtub doors caught my attention. Something dark, sitting just below the porcelain surface.

I slowly pushed the left glass door open, peeking inside.

And found Donna Martinez staring up at me with vacant eyes.

Dead.

CHAPTER TEN

───────

Danny scratched his chin. "Her husband died, she sought revenge on the judge, and then killed herself. What a life."

Regardless of how long I stared at her, Donna's sunken eyes and deadpan stare continued to chill me as sharply as it had when I'd first seen her, screamed, and jumped back about fifteen feet from her body. Her eyes were glassy, her skin blue, the slack muscles in her face reminding me of a wax doll. She wore yellow bunny pajamas and matching fuzzy slippers, which led me to believe she'd been there awhile. Even actresses were up and dressed by noon.

I shivered again, despite the jacket Danny had thrown over my shoulders. I was a P.I. who dealt with sex. Give me a spouse cheating with the maid, cheating with the nanny, cheating with the frickin yoga instructor. Not a stiff.

I squeezed my eyes shut and took a few deep breaths. I could do this. I was a big girl. It was just a dead body. No biggie, right?

I opened them again, trying to see the room without the cloud of squick factor. Two empty prescription bottles, one of generic hydrocodone and the other of Tylenol with Codeine, sat in Donna's lap. Several pills were scattered around her body, as if she'd meant to take them, but they'd fallen from her hands or mouth. Her body was slumped in an uncomfortable position, though how much of that was post-mortem, I had no idea. Her head lay under the faucet, her feet tucked underneath her.

I narrowed my eyes. Who sat in the tub in that direction?

"No. This doesn't feel right."

"What do you mean?" Danny asked.

"She was angry at Judge Waterston for sending Miguel to his death in prison so she kills him, sets me up, and then swallows a bunch of pills? It took a whole lot of anger to fuel that murder. Angry people don't suddenly go apathetic and kill themselves. I mean, why not go after the inmate who killed Miguel? The prosecutor who put him away? The public defender who failed?"

I stepped back and stared at the walls and ceiling, waiting for my broken thoughts to piece into a cohesive puzzle.

"Besides, look at this place. The furnishings, the colors and patterns. Does she seem like a woman who concocted an elaborate scheme to not only shoot the judge but also plant me as a suspect?"

"Since when does color scheme have to do a person's intelligence?" Danny asked, eyebrows furrowing together.

"Not the colors exactly," I explained. "But everything just seems so simple here. So plucked from a magazine. She doesn't strike me as the type who has a whole lot of original or creative thoughts."

Danny bit the inside of his cheek. "So... you think she was working with someone else?"

I'll admit, I hadn't been sure, just processing out loud. But Danny's question sharpened my suspicions.

"Or *for* someone else. Someone hired her to play a part." It made perfect sense.

Danny stared at the body, uncertainty splattered all over his expression. "Okay. Let's assume she was. Someone knows she's an actress, knows she doesn't exactly have a deep love of the judge. So, they hire her to play Mrs. Waterston and get you involved."

"And once she sets me up, she kills the judge."

Danny looked down at the woman in the tub again. "But something must have gone wrong. The partner gets nervous."

"Or Donna gets greedy," I added, picking up his train of thought. "Either way, it's not safe to keep her around anymore."

"So he kills her, then makes it look like a suicide."

I nodded. "Now, if the cops get hold of me, there's absolutely no one to back up my 'crazy story' about a fake wife hiring me to spy on her husband. This guy gets away with it. Again. His second murder."

Danny nodded. "It's a theory," he hedged.

"Who gets in the tub and puts their head up against the faucet?" I pointed for emphasis. "Who lies in their bathtub to take pills? Why not her bed or the couch? Spend her last moments in comfort, staring at Miguel's photo. People die in tubs after slitting their wrists, and not while wearing fuzzy slippers."

"So now what do we do?" Danny asked.

I let out a breath. Honestly? I didn't know. My leads had just died with Donna. And the knowledge that we ransacked her place while she was lying there dead left a new unsettled feeling in the pit of my stomach.

Great detective work, Jamie.

"Let's get out of here."

As I blamed myself for not being a bloodhound, we hurried through the living room. I opened the front door and poked my head out. I half expected cop cars to come screaming to the curb, but the sidewalk was empty; even the traffic had died. I thanked God for small favors.

We dashed across the street and back into the van. The last thing I needed was my face plastered across the six o'clock news for another murder.

The humidity inside the van instantly bathed my body in a fine sheen of perspiration. Danny had covered the vinyl seats with fake fur since stake-outs were synonymous with baking our internal organs or freezing off our extremities, depending on the time of year.

I grabbed my phone, ready to call Aiden, and realized I held my Smartphone. I'd left the prepaid back at the office.

"Find a pay phone."

Danny turned and gave me a look. "What is this, nineteen-eighty? *Are* there any payphones left in L.A.?"

I flipped him the bird. "Fine. Find a mini-mart where I can get a pre-paid."

He started the car, still grinning at me as he made a left at the corner, then drove two more blocks before finding a gas station with a convenience store attached. I threw on a pair of sunglasses and tucked my hair into a bun, keeping my head down as I quickly went inside, bought the cheapest pre-paid cell they had with cash, then ducked out.

"Who are you calling?" Danny asked.

"The ADA. Someone has to report the body."

I could hear his disapproval in the silence even before I looked up from my dialing to see the grim set of his jaw.

"Why not call nine-one-one?" he asked.

"Because this is personal."

His brows creased, and his eyes darkened. He didn't understand, and I didn't have time to explain.

I listened to the phone ring three times before Aiden picked up.

"Prince?"

"It's Jamie." There wasn't any time for small talk. Far from an expert on corpses, I wasn't sure how long Donna had been in the tub, but I knew it was only a matter of time before her neighbors would be wondering what had died in the walls.

He didn't respond, and I wondered if I'd lost the connection.

"Are you there?"

A door clicked shut in the background. "Yes. You ran out on me before…"

Before I could be arrested? Yeah, sorry, pal. "Listen. There's a dead body."

"What?"

I rattled off the address.

"Who lives there?"

A car pulled into the lot beside us. Instinctively I ducked down below the window.

"Donna Martinez," I answered.

A mother and child got out of the car next door, paying zero attention to me.

"Who is Donna Martinez?" Aiden asked.

Admitting how I knew Donna entailed explaining a whole lot more than I was willing to share at the moment.

"Jamie?" he prodded.

"She's in the tub," I told him. "I found her like that, but I had nothing to do with her death."

"Like you had nothing to do with Judge Waterston's murder?"

I swallowed hard. So the cat and mouse thing was over. Cards were being laid on the table. I wasn't sure if I was relieved or more anxious.

"Exactly," I slowly agreed.

Aiden paused. "Are your prints going to be in Ms. Martinez's house?" he asked.

I bit my lip. "My prints?" In order to have a fingerprint to match he'd have to know...

"James Bond, licensed private investigator, prints on file with the state of California."

I closed my eyes and thought a really dirty word. I'd known it was only a matter of time before he figured it out, but I'd hoped for more. I pictured his army of police officers at the agency right now, combing through records, asking Maya where her boss was, digging through my computer for any mention of Waterston. I shook off the panic that accompanied that vision, focusing on the voice on the other end of the pre-paid.

"How did you find out?"

"You were careful not to touch your martini glass last night, but as you jumped up from the table, you grabbed the butter knife."

Damn.

Danny shot me a look. Clearly he could tell from my end of things, this conversation was not going well.

"Okay, so you know who I am and what I do. Would you believe this is all about a client and not about me killing anyone?"

There was radio silence on the other end. I held my breath.

"I believe in evidence," he said slowly. "I believe what I can prove in court."

It was a typical lawyer's answer. Full of words while saying nothing. But if I read between the lines, he wasn't exactly convinced of my guilt either.

"I didn't do this," I said point blank. "I'm being set up."

Again Aiden was slow to respond, as if carefully measuring his words before speaking. "I've been reading up on your history today. About your agency. You don't strike me as the careless type. If your background is any indication, if you murdered someone, you'd make certain there wasn't any photographic evidence lying around, let alone being aired on TV."

"Thank you," I breathed, letting out a breath I'd been holding for two days. Though I wasn't entirely sure it was a compliment, it was as close as the lawyer in him was going to get to telling me he wasn't out for my blood.

Yet.

"Where are you, Jamie?" he asked.

I bit my lip. I'd been on the phone for awhile now. Too long. Even with a pre-paid, Aiden could ping a cell tower and get a location on me.

"I have to go," I said.

"Wait! I... I want to help you."

God, I wanted to believe that. I looked from Danny to the phone.

"I need to hear your side of things," Aiden continued. "In person."

"Meet in person?"

Danny shook his head, mouthing the word, "no".

"I can help you, Jamie," Aiden said again. "but I need you to trust me."

"I fell for that once," I pointed out. "You had cops waiting for me last night."

"Don't do it," Danny whispered.

"I promise I won't involve anyone else," Aiden reassured me. "Just you and me. You can pick the place this time."

Now I was on the phone *way* too long. I needed to get off. The woman and the kid reemerged from the store, the bell above the glass door jiggling loudly enough to give me a mild heart attack.

"Fine," I said.

Danny scoffed and ran his hand through his hair.

I turned my back to him, not wanting to hear the negatives. I knew this was a stupid idea. I knew I couldn't trust Aiden, even if part of me really wanted to. But what choice did I have? I'd been named, fingerprinted. I was running out of places to turn. If I didn't play nice with the ADA, I could count my moments of freedom on one hand. At least this way I bought myself a little more time.

"I'll meet you tonight," I promised, and rattled off an address before quickly hanging up the cell.

CHAPTER ELEVEN

———

"Are you insane?" Danny yelled in my ear as soon as he started the van again.

An older man pumping gas glanced our way.

I slumped down in my seat and glared at Danny. "Shut up, and drive to the agency."

He matched my glare but pulled onto the road.

I knew no place was safe now, not the office, not my apartment. But I needed to get my car. Assuming it hadn't been impounded and logged as evidence by now.

Danny kept his attention on the road and a death grip on the steering wheel until we'd put several blocks between us and Donna's apartment. It wasn't until we were merging back onto the freeway that he turned to me. "So, want to tell me why you're doing this?"

"Going to the agency? I need my car."

"No! Jesus, Jamie. Setting a *date* with the ADA."

I leaned forward, cranking up the A/C. The forced air cooled off my face and neck and gave me a moment to think clearly. "He knows who I am."

"I gathered that," Danny conceded.

"I'm buying myself some time."

"So you have no intention of keeping this date?"

I didn't answer right away.

"James..." Danny warned.

I jerked toward him as much as the seatbelt allowed. "Look he knows who I am and what I do. Don't you think it's a good idea if I find out what else he knows?"

"No," he said, emphatically.

"What if he has info about the judge? About how he was killed or the murder weapon or something else that could give us a hint who Donna was working for? In case you haven't noticed, we're at a big fat zero for leads."

Danny clenched his teeth together. But he didn't yell, which I took as a good sign.

"Look, I distrust Aiden as much as you do-" I continued.

"I doubt that!" Danny spat back.

But I let it go.

"-but I'm out of other ideas. If he can help-"

"Help?" Danny jumped on me again. "I thought you said the plan was to milk him for info, not throw yourself on the mercy of the DA's office."

"I don't *throw* myself anywhere," I countered. "But if Aiden does believe me, maybe he can do something."

Danny turned on me, steam practically pouring from his ears. "You're nuts, you know that?"

I threw my hands up. "Isn't this exactly what you and Levine were cooking up for me to do last night? Turn myself in, talk to the ADA?"

"I wasn't cooking up anything," he countered. "I was trying to help your sorry ass stay out of jail."

"Gee, my hero," I said, sarcasm dripping from my words.

"Besides, that was before."

"Before what?"

"Before *both* of our prints ended up all over the apartment of a murdered woman."

I bit my lip, realizing how true that was. "I'm sorry I dragged you into this."

Danny shook his head, let out a deep breath. "Christ, that's not what I meant, and you know it."

"What I know is that I'm tired of looking over my shoulder, Danny. I need to find the person behind all of this, so I can get back to pleasant work, like spying on cheating husbands. I need some peace, some quiet, and a full night's sleep."

"Yeah, well the way you're going, it will be in a five by six cell," he shot back.

We pulled up to Bond Agency, behind my car, which, thankfully, was unassaulted by the cops.

So far.

Danny cut the engine and turned to me. "Look, this whole meeting thing is stupid and dangerous."

"I need to go."

"I won't be a part of it," he warned.

I narrowed my eyes at him. This entire conversation had left a bad taste in my mouth, and this was the last straw. I flung open the door and jumped out.

"You know what, that's great. It's just fine with me. In fact, stay away from me. I don't need you tonight."

Something flashed in his eyes, but it was gone too quickly for me to register the emotion.

"You can't go in without protection."

"Oh, I never said that. I simply said I don't need *you*. I've got my girls. *Them*, I can count on."

I slammed the door and stomped to my car.

* * *

I spent the afternoon driving, seething, and grasping at anything to help me indentify Donna's killer. Thankful I had the new cell, and I called Maya to run every cross check she could against Donna and the judge, fishing for a common third party. Of course, her resources were a bit limited, the police having taken over the office by then, but she did her best on a Wifi connection on her laptop at the Starbucks down the street. Caleigh went to work on trying to reconstruct Donna's last movements, posing as a friend of the deceased from "back home" as she chatted with neighbors, friends, and casting agents. And Sam set up surveillance on Donna's apartment, trying to keep tabs on what the police found. By the time sunset peaked over the hills, I'd exhausted every avenue I could think of, but unfortunately was no closer to the truth. Leaving me just one alternative.

Aiden.

Danny was right. It was gutsy bordering on stupid to meet him again. Especially when he'd had police ready to nab me at the restaurant. But I was just desperate enough to ignore the stupid part and bank on gutsy.

I'd told Aiden to meet me in Chaplin Park, a small, neighborhood spot in Burbank, tucked between studios and streets lined with fifties-style bungalows left over from Hollywood's golden era. Nine o'clock. Under the gazebo in the center.

Eight-forty-six I showed up and sat on a bench hidden behind a grove of trees. I did a slow sweep of the park, ascertaining that the street lamps and I were alone. I looked up, seeing the one lone star bright enough to shine through the smog layer. I had a crazy urge to make a childish wish on it.

Please, wishing star, keep me from being arrested and wrongfully imprisoned tonight.

I fidgeted on the cool, smooth wood and looked down into my blouse to make sure the mic was well hidden. There was no camera tonight. Not in the dark. Besides, I only needed to record Aiden's words. There would be nothing to video out here.

Caleigh and Sam were parked down the road in Sam's beat-up Dodge Neon. It was less conspicuous than my Roadster or Caleigh's Ford Taurus. When they picked me up, Sam didn't look well. She'd ended up taking her son with her to stake out Donna's when the sitter came down with a stomach virus. Two hours in a hot car with a bored ten-year-old sounded less enjoyable than having a wisdom tooth extracted. I did not envy her. But, I was grateful that she'd done it. In Sam's world not getting the job done was up there with running into her ex in the toilet paper aisle of Costco while wearing sweat pants and mismatched sneakers. Just one more reason I didn't want to fire her.

A twig snapped, and I honed in on a figure approaching from the parking lot. I had expected him to be wearing another tailored suit, highly professional and coiffed. Instead he was in a pair of casual blue jeans and a black T-shirt. The change in attire took me off guard for a moment, and I suddenly wondered if it was intended to do just that.

"The street's clear. He seems to be alone," Caleigh whispered in my ear, as he approached the gazebo.

He looked around, scanning the park as I'd done. Clearly he didn't see me, as he shoved his hands in his pockets and sat on a white bench in the gazebo. Though I noticed that he perched on the edge. He was as antsy as I was.

I took a couple of deep breaths. It was now or never.

I slowly got up, stepped carefully out of the shadows, and made my way toward Aiden.

He heard me approaching and looked up, a smile that I could have sworn held genuine pleasure lighting his features under the dim glow of the streetlamps.

"Jamie," he spoke, standing as I entered the gazebo. Ever the gentleman.

"Aiden."

He nodded to the bench beside him. "I'm glad you agreed to this."

"I hope I didn't make a mistake." I sat beside him, careful to keep distance between us.

"You didn't." There was that confidence again.

"So, you know who I am."

He nodded. "I'm curious," he said, cocking his head to the side. "What makes someone go from runway model to private investigator? It's a big switch."

I shrugged. "You'd be surprised how often the two jobs call for the same skill set."

"Like catching the eye of the judge at the benefit dinner."

Right to the point.

I inhaled, catching a whiff of his musky aftershave, as I prepared to take a gamble and lay my cards on the table. "His wife, or rather, the woman posing as his wife, hired me to get proof her husband was cheating."

"And did you?"

"Yes. Only the woman I gave it to wasn't really Mrs. Waterston. It was Donna Martinez.

"So, that's the link. Donna posed as the wife and hired you to bust the judge?"

"Yes." I paused. "But someone hired her to hire me."

He raised en eyebrow.

"Look, I know this is starting to sound like a conspiracy theory, but, well..." I paused, biting my lip, not having felt this nervous since my second grade spelling bee. "It is. A conspiracy, I mean. Someone went to a lot of trouble to frame me."

"Why?" Aiden asked, his tone flat, even, not betraying the slightest hint of belief or disbelief.

"I wish I knew."

He digested this for a moment. "Ms. Martinez. She paid you for your services?"

"Cash. Not traceable."

"That's not odd?"

"Not in my business."

"Anything else you can tell me about her?" he asked, clearly fishing for something, though I wasn't sure what.

I shrugged. "Honestly, she looked like every other wife I deal with daily. She was considerably younger than him, but if that's a crime, half of L.A. would be arrested."

A corner of his mouth lifted. "True."

"Infidelity is a private investigator's specialty. Our bread and butter."

"The police usually handle murder."

"And I'd gladly let them if they weren't accusing *me*." Irritation filled my tone.

He stared at me, eyes unreadable. I noticed his demeanor was much less affable than it had been at dinner last night. All pretense of flirtation was gone, his witty banter replaced with bare facts. Even so, I felt a current of something running just under his words. His eyes lingered a little too long on my hemline, his body language just a little too relaxed, words drawled a little too slowly. Whether it was unintentional or by design to make me uncomfortable, I wasn't sure. But I felt myself shifting under his gaze, heat filling my cheeks. Open leering I was used to. Occupational hazard. But this slow, assessment, flirting with the border of sensual and clinical, was new.

"So when did you realize Donna Martinez was not what she seemed?" he asked.

I cleared my throat. "When I saw the real wife on the news."

He nodded, pieces clicking into place. "Along with the video of you."

I nodded back at him in agreement. "We tracked the package the video was delivered in to Donna."

"I thought it was an anonymous delivery?"

"It was, but we found her through the stationary."

The corner of his mouth hitched up. "Clever."

I thought so, but now wasn't the time to gloat. Instead I cleared my throat again. "Okay, I've shown you mine, now show my yours."

The smiled hitched higher, definitely falling closer to the sensual side of the border. "Mine?"

"Everything the reporters on TV are saying points to me. But you must have other evidence, or else I'd be in handcuffs right now," I pointed out with a lot more bravado than I felt.

Aiden shook his head. "I'm sorry, there's not much I can tell you. It's an ongoing investigation."

I felt my teeth grind. "But you believe me?" I asked, hating just how desperately I wanted him to say yes.

Like the lawyer he was, he didn't answer.

"I don't like to lose," he said. "I want my ducks in a row before I go in front of a jury."

I gave him a hard stare, wondering just what ducks he was trying to line up tonight.

As if to answer my question, he followed that up with, "When was the last time you saw Donna Martinez alive?"

I shook my head slowly. "You haven't shown me yours, yet," I pointed out.

He might have been annoyed, but instead that slow smile spread across his face again, this time even touching his eyes. "Okay, I can play fair. The medical examiner says Donna Martinez died of an overdose of an amphetamine-type stimulant. It wasn't any of the pills she had a prescription for. There's no sign of forced entry or anything to conclude she hadn't taken them voluntarily."

"Wait-" I said, holding up a hand. "If the pills in her system were not prescription, then they weren't the ones I saw scattered around her body?"

The smile widened. "Beautiful and smart. No. The pills we found with the body were not in her system. They were similar, likely having caused a similar effect. And, had there not been extenuating circumstances-"

"Me finding her and linking her to the judge," I supplied.

He nodded. "-we likely never would have tested them as closely as we did."

"She would have just been written off as a suicide. A woman distraught over the death of her husband."

Aiden nodded again in the soft light. "Something like that."

I paused, taking this all in. "But why not just kill her with the pills she had on hand?"

"Painkillers mostly, given to her by her dentist after extracting a molar, six months ago. They could have killed her in a significant enough dosage, but it would have taken some time. Enough, possibly, for her to realize she was in trouble and call for help. There were no ligature marks on the body, no sign of restraint."

"That would have raised a red flag with the police," I mused.

"Exactly. Whoever administered the stuff needed to do so in a way that she'd willingly take it, then never know what hit her. Which is exactly what the tox screen showed."

"So, what drug did kill her?"

"Designer club drug. Though, her system showed levels far above anything we've seen coming into the ER in party-goers. They call it Shooting Stars, and my sources in vice say it's costly."

"Not something a struggling actress could afford," I pointed out.

"No."

Relief should've flooded through me. I was right. There was a mastermind behind all of this who had killed Donna. And Aiden knew it. But the look on his face wasn't as reassuring as I'd like.

"So this means I'm cleared?"

His laid-back expression twitched. "Donna's death is being ruled murder. But I have no physical evidence linking her to the judge."

"But you said-"

"*Physical evidence,*" he repeated.

Shit. He was right. The stationary only proved that Donna *could* have been the one to send the video to the police station. Not how she got it or why. And the drugs only proved she was killed by someone, not who, not that it wasn't me, not that it had anything to do with the judge.

Aiden leaned forward, closing some of the distance between us. "Look, I want to believe you, Jamie," he said, his voice low and softer now. "I really do."

I swallowed hard, his sudden foray into tenderness surprising me.

"But you can't," I answered.

He slowly shook his head back and forth, the apology in his eyes clear. "I wouldn't be doing my job if I ignored evidence."

"I'm not asking you to ignore," I countered. "Just... keep an open mind."

"I'm here, aren't I?"

I nodded. He was. Though I still wasn't quite sure why.

"Jamie, I'm sorry," he started, leaning just that much closer. His eyes shone under the lamplight, a brilliant blue. His mouth softened, his eyebrows drawing together in genuine concern.

As he opened his mouth to say more, I felt myself softening in response.

But he stopped there.

An unmistakable wee-ooh sound of sirens blared through the night air, shattering the calm.

For one second our eyes locked.

"Oh, we got trouble, Jamie," Caleigh said in my ear.

Fury snaked up my back, clenching my muscles, making me tremble. This wasn't happening. Not again.

I jumped up at the same time as Aiden.

He reached toward me.

Did he expect to hold me down, wrestle me to the ground so the police could arrive and cuff me? He had another thing coming.

I curled my fist and swung.

CHAPTER TWELVE

My heels seeped deep into the sand at the playground. It slowed me down, making each step more difficult. My thigh muscles ached, but I wasn't stopping. Sirens blasted from the west, so I booked it east.

And I wasn't alone.

Aiden, after recovering from my right hook straight to his eye, followed me. I felt him a few steps behind. He called my name as I rounded the seesaw, but I didn't turn around.

Perspiration pressed my blouse to my back and dotted my forehead. My ear piece fell out somewhere near the slide. The mic jiggled between my boobs.

"I'm exiting near the swings," I yelled into my chest, gasping for air, in case they could hear me.

Hopefully Aiden couldn't.

My main thought, *I can't believe I let him trick me again*, pumped adrenaline through my legs and kept me moving.

By the time I neared the exit, flashing red and blue lights illuminated the night sky. They were too close. Aiden's slapping footsteps gained distance. I considered kicking off my pumps, but a) they were snakeskin, b) they cost way too much to leave on the side of the road, and c) running barefoot on cement and pebbles was painful.

My lungs burned. My pulse pounded in my ears, competing with the sirens. The sandy ground turned into concrete, and I lunged forward, gaining new momentum. My skin burned. I wanted to shrug it off. I would've settled for removing my jacket, but my gun was still holstered to my side. It was the last thing the police needed to see.

The Welcome and Please Don't Litter signs blurred as I ran past. Once I hit the street, I stopped for a second to gather my wits. Perspiration slid into my eye. I pushed it away with the back of my hand. The blue and red lights were up ahead, by the west entrance. Could they see me?

Cars sped down the road. There was no sign of the girls. Knowing Aiden was a step behind, I darted across the street. Horns blasted, but I couldn't take the time to cross safely. I headed east, knowing the area somewhat well.

I weaved around a couple holding hands, a group of teenagers smoking cigarettes, and a homeless guy begging for change. I neared the corner and charged forward, hoping that once I turned I'd have a moment to hide and get Aiden off my tail. I didn't look back, didn't want to see how close he was, but I knew he was still back there. I sensed his proximity.

As I leaned into the turn, a man appeared, and I plowed into him.

I lost my breath and bounced off his chest, like a rag doll. Instead of landing on my back, I twisted and fell into a bicycle propped against the store front.

We both slid to the ground. Me and the bike. Not me and the man. The man kept going, never stopping to see if I was okay, or if a handlebar was jammed into my ribs.

Rude much?

I sprawled across the metal hunk of junk. My palms scraped the sidewalk, but my left knee took most of the brunt, stuck between the wheel spokes. Bolts of fire shot into my thigh. On the verge of tears, I wanted to cry, scream and throw a two-year-old tantrum.

I didn't have time to nurse my bruises though, physical or emotional. Self-preservation brought me to my knees. Indecent, manly grunts tore from my chest as I climbed to my feet. I wobbled around the corner, hoping my leg wouldn't cramp. I hurried around a woman shouting into her cell and turned to the neon red sign in my peripheral vision.

The Spotted Pony.

Exhilaration spread through my weary bones. How could I forget this place was here?

I limped across the street with a smile. The girls and I worked a case here six months ago. A near-hysterical wife hired us to get the goods on her husband who was frequenting the club. She suspected he was sleeping with a dancer named Luscious Lavender. After a week of stake-outs and an offer from the owner to dance, we discovered the man had been married previously. He'd lost touch with his first wife, who fled from the relationship three months pregnant. Luscious Lavender was the guy's daughter.

I pushed open the heavy wooden door and rushed inside. No one manned the entrance, so I sprinted into the club mindful that Aiden and his cop parade could barge through at any moment.

I slipped to the left, trying to blend in with the horny crowd. The woman on stage hung upside down, with her legs wrapped around a pole. Several young guys in the front row cheered and barked. It was either a bachelor party or their first time.

I spotted Omar, the owner, near the bar and shouted his name. I limped over, panting like a wild dog.

He looked up and chuckled, recognizing me immediately. At six-feet, two-hundred and fifty pounds and sporting a military buzz, he resembled a bouncer more than an entrepreneur. He took in my limp and my labored breaths and uttered one word. "Who?"

"GQ," is all I got out between pants. Damn, I needed to work out more.

I barely heard the door swing open above the house music and cat calls, but I sensed him. I stepped to the side and used Omar as a human shield.

"Candy, Apple." He snapped his fingers and pointed to Aiden.

Immediately two girls working the tables jumped to attention. They were dressed in halters and skirts so short their butt cheeks were visible from beneath. Strapped to their freshly pedicured feet were glittery stilettos. They slithered over to Aiden. The pale one pressed her man-made tits to his bicep. The other leaned into him and gyrated against his hip. If I wasn't running for my life, I would've enjoyed watching him squirm away.

Omar kissed the top of my head. "I saw your picture on the news. Clear yourself and be safe."

Without another word, he turned his back and continued playing guard as I snuck alongside the stage to the back offices.

I appreciated that he never asked if I killed the judge.

Chatter and laughter from the dressing area grew louder as the music softened. Light spilled onto the tarnished wood floor, and I stopped at the adjacent door. I peeked in.

Three girls were applying liquid eyeliner and brushing their hair. Luscious Lavender had stopped working here after her father insisted she come live with him and his wife. I heard she enrolled in the dental hygiene program at the community college. His wife ended up filing for divorce. Despite the biological connection, she couldn't stand another woman in her husband's life.

I turned away and stepped into Omar's cool, dark office, a momentary reprieve, and walked around his desk.

During my time staking out Luscious Lavender and Daddy, I'd spent several hours working the floor. Not the stage. Serving drinks, ignoring roaming hands on my butt, and making decent tips.

When Omar discovered I was a PI, and I never did find out just how, he dragged me into his office and demanded I spill. I had, he'd laughed, then he'd agreed to let me stay as long as I needed, even showing me his secret back door exit to the alleyway in case I needed a quick escape.

The exact route I took now.

As I threw open the door, the balmy night air hitting me square in the face, I heard tires screech around the corner. A second later, Caleigh and Sam pulled to a stop at the back door and waved me over.

Perfect timing.

Caleigh opened the passenger door and scooted toward the glove compartment. I pushed up the back of her seat and squeezed in.

Sam smiled at me through the rearview mirror, but she spoke to Caleigh. "See, I knew she'd head for The Spotted Pony."

Damned, now I really didn't want to fire her.

I leaned my head back as Sam took a left out of the alley, heading toward the freeway. I closed my eyes willing my heart rate to return to normal. I needed a long, hot shower and a cold, stiff drink.

* * *

We pulled up in front of Maya's. The office was off-limits, as was my apartment, and we needed answers fast. When we stepped through the doorway of her apartment, she was pouring four, large margaritas on the rocks. God, I loved her.

I limped to the upholstered sofa and flopped onto it. My knee throbbed, and it was all I could do to not clench my teeth and bellow warrior style.

Maya handed me a drink and held out two bottles. One was over-the-counter, generic ibuprofen and the other was prescribed Oxycodone. "From when I had kidney stones last year," she explained.

I grabbed the amber bottle, popped a giant white pill into my mouth and gulped the 'rita. Cold, frothy and with extra tequila. God bless alcohol.

I'd only been here twice. The first time when Maya moved in and the second to celebrate her twenty-fifth birthday. The second time I'd been declared the designated driver.

Luckily I wasn't driving tonight.

Everything looked the same. Glass accent tables, navy upholstery, a few simple picture frames and no unnecessary clutter. A sleek glass and metal desk sat across from the couch. Her laptop displayed a Google results page. Obviously she'd already begun searching.

That was my girl.

Sam and Caleigh settled in with their drinks, and I closed my eyes for a moment. I pushed thoughts of Aiden aside and focused on which would soothe my pain first, the alcohol or medication.

"How's Julio?" Maya asked Sam.

"He's fine. It's the babysitter that can't stop puking. A neighbor's watching him tonight, but she's not available tomorrow."

With everything going on, it would've been easy to tell her to stay home with her kid. They each deserved a day off. But even if I ignored the murder charge hanging over my head, there was still the matter of a failing business. We couldn't afford to lose any clients, and I couldn't afford to lose one of my girls.

"I did a reverse lookup on that number you got from Donna's place, boss," Maya said.

I opened my eyes and sat up, trying not to wince and show my enormous discomfort. "And?"

She pressed her lips together and shook her head. "It led to an optometrist's office. Donna had an eye exam scheduled for next week."

I sighed. Another dead end.

Maya turned to her computer. "But I've been digging for info on the drug - Shooting Stars."

"And?" I asked, taking another sip.

"From what I could find, there seems to be a lot of chatter about it on *Twitter*. It's in code for the most part. Here, look."

She clicked several keys and pulled up the account of someone named Sgrbabee69. The profile picture showed a barely legal young woman with glitter eye shadow and frosted lipstick.

Maya pointed to the statuses. "She's talking to some guy about getting together and watching for shooting stars."

"Does she give any clue where they go to get the stuff?" I asked.

Maya refreshed the page and read the words, mumbling out loud. The print was too small for me to see, and I wasn't ready to give up my comfortable position.

"Last weekend they met at Club Dante."

Invisible icy fingers trailed along my spine. "Donna worked there."

How likely was it a coincidence? Not that it mattered. I didn't believe in coincidences.

"So that's where I go." I braced the arm and back of the sofa to use as leverage as I stood up. The throbbing in my knee wasn't as strong as before, but the room teetered to the left.

"Whoa." I slid back onto the cushion. Margarita sloshed onto my skirt.

"Yeah, you're not going anywhere now, boss." Sam took the glass from my hand and set it on the coffee table.

"I don't have time to rest."

"Too bad. You won't make it otherwise."

As much as I wanted to disagree further, I knew I was in no condition to do anything more than sleep. The only problem was where.

As if reading my mind, Maya said, "You can stay here."

I shook my head slowly, fearing sudden movements. "No, thank you. It'll just be a matter of minutes before they search for me at all of your places. I shouldn't even be here now."

"Well you can't go home, so what? A motel?" Caleigh wrinkled her nose at the idea. Unless it offered chocolate mints on your pillow cases and had a concierge, she deemed the place inferior.

Too bad my wallet couldn't appreciate her tastes.

Danny's place was completely out of the question, too. Not only because of the police, but I was still pissed at him and had no intention of admitting he was right about tonight. No, I needed a hideaway off the radar, with someone no one would suspect.

A tidal wave of nausea, not due to my dangerous combination of narcotics and alcohol, consumed me.

Damn.

Derek.

CHAPTER THIRTEEN

Daylight streamed through the port holes, stabbing me awake. I pushed my face into the pillow and groaned. Did the man not believe in shades?

After wobbling along the pier in my snakeskins last night, I'd found Derek in a "loving" embrace with a bottle-blonde wearing more make-up than Bozo the Clown. Trying to avert my eyes, I'd asked, "Can I crash here until I clear my name?"

His reply: "Knock yourself out, kid."

Luckily that had been the extent of our conversation. I had a feeling he was saving the real interrogation for this morning, when he was sober(ish) and alone.

While Aiden and his crew would know full well that Derek was biologically linked to me, it would take a little more digging to find my dad. As a P.I., Derek had always believed in living off the radar - P.O. Box for all his mail, no home phone, utilities in a corporate name. The harder it was for an angry husband to find him the better, he'd always told me. And his security obsession had only grown after getting shot. Making the boat registered to a 'Captain Jack Sparrow, Inc.' (Derek always did have a sense of humor) the perfect secure hideout.

The delicious aroma of dark roast weaved its way around my dull senses, awakening me further. I shrugged off the covers and stretched. After Derek had welcomed me aboard, the captain and I hadn't spoken a word. Which meant this was the big moment. No messages to delete, no screened calls, no egg timer.

I sighed and headed to the bathroom. My headache was light, and the throbbing in my knee had gone down, but I still limped. There'd be no chasing unfaithful husbands for me for a few days.

I splashed water on my face and noticed an unopened, packaged toothbrush. I couldn't help a grin. Why did I get the feeling Derek was used to unexpected overnight guests?

I tore open the package and squeezed white paste onto the bristles. After feeling a bit more human, I hobbled toward the scent of coffee and found a full pot in the galley. On the counter, nestled between the microwave and a box of Cap'n Crunch sat a coffee can of fresh cut wildflowers.

The same ones at Mom's grave.

A sudden wave of nostalgia hit me. After Mom had died, Derek had refused to talk about her. Even though I was young at the time, I'd understood somehow that it was just too painful. But as the initial shock and pain had subsided some for me, morphing into a dull sense of loss that never quite went away, it had frustrated me that no one ever mentioned her. But Derek had stood fast. She was gone, and that was all there was to say on the matter. I guess over the years I'd just stopped associating Derek with my mom. The small reminder that he still thought of her was comforting. Okay, maybe the guy wasn't all bad.

I poured a cup and sat at the table, gazing out to sea.

Small waves rippled the water. Over the horizon, the sun rose, coloring the grey sky with strokes of orange and yellow. It looked like another horrendously hot day approaching.

Giggles pinpricked the quiet.

I sucked in a breath. Great. Bottle-blonde was still here.

I grabbed my coffee and started toward the cabins when Derek appeared in the doorway.

"Morning," he grumbled then reached for my mug, taking a healthy swig. Hair tousled, dressed in shorts and tank, he didn't look ready to tackle the day. And I definitely didn't want to spend the day with a bear.

Another giggle sounded, and I turned to find Elaine, from the news station, in the doorway. Her hair was mussed, her make-up smudged on one side, and her cheek bore a wrinkled pillow impression. In person, she was shorter than she appeared on camera. Kinda like the reverse effect of a car's side view mirror.

I looked away, trying with all my might not to imagine the two of them together.

"Don't mind him," she said with a smirk. "He's always grouchy before the first cup, which is why I showed him how to operate the machine's automatic timer."

How domestic of them.

He waved away her words and gulped the hot liquid. Like a super hero in a phone booth, he went from scary, old geezer to attractive, old man in seconds. He stood taller and more alert. He smiled at us, looking from one to the other. "Elaine, this is James."

"Jamie," I corrected automatically.

She extended her squat arm and wrapped her hand around mine. "Good to meet you. He talks about you all the time."

I raised an eyebrow in his direction. "Really?"

She widened her eyes, giving off an innocent look, but I doubted there was anything naïve about this woman. "Oh yes. He's always mentioning the agency. Wondering how it's going."

I smirked. "Yes, his love for the cases is exceptionally touching."

He shot me a look, then handed me back my mug (empty) and reached into the cupboard for one of his own.

Elaine glanced at her watch. "Well, I need to get to my place to change before work. It was super nice meeting you though, James."

"Jamie."

She ignored me, turning her attention to the captain, murmuring some thankfully unintelligible sweet talk that had even Derek blushing by the time she was done.

I poured myself a fresh cup, headed back to the table, sat down and stared at the water, trying to block out the scene.

Giggles and wet lip smacking erupted that reminded me of junior high braces, sneaking under the bleachers, and heading back to class chewing flavorless gum that wasn't mine. Ick.

I rolled my eyes and considered throwing myself overboard.

"Call you later," Elaine finally promised.

I turned in time to catch Derek playfully slap her on the butt.

She walked out, and Derek sat opposite me at the table.

"How's the leg?" he asked. "That limp seemed bad last night."

"Fine."

"Want to tell me what happened?"

"No."

"So, what's going on with the Martin case?"

I rested my head on the table. This would be the longest day of my life. "Don't you have something to do?"

Someone else to torture.

"Are you kidding? This is the first time I get to spend time with my daughter, and she can't escape or ignore her phone. Do you think I'd pass it up by running errands?" The mocking seriousness of his tone made the hairs on the back of neck prickle.

"I have more pressing issues than the Martins at the moment," I mumbled in response.

Derek stared at me a beat. Then nodded. "I know, James."

I ducked my head, really not ready to have this conversation without another cup of coffee. Which, by the way, I had to hand it to Miss Trix, was really good.

"She makes good coffee," I said, doing a lame attempt at subject change

Derek nodded again. "She does. Elaine's a good woman."

I held my breath and waited for the sexual innuendo, but it never arrived. Sitting up straight, I brought the mug to my lips and took a long sip.

"You really like her, don't you?"

"Nice try, kid. We were talking about you. And your legal troubles."

Damn. He was good.

Just then footsteps sounded on the dock.

My heart leapt, and I froze. I stared wide-eyed at Derek, who was on his feet and out the door in a flash. Voices sounded. I couldn't make out any words, but one sounded higher. A woman? I prayed that Elaine had forgotten something and that Aiden hadn't sent a female officer after me.

The footsteps grew closer. Two pairs? Three? I couldn't tell. Derek wouldn't allow the cops to search his boat without a warrant, would he?

Suddenly a boy in long, baggy shorts and an Angry Birds T-shirt jumped into the room. A backpack draped over his right shoulder, he clutched a portable game system in his hand.

Julio.

"Hey, Aunt Jamie," he said, then plopped across from me.

Derek entered a beat later with Sam. "Look what I found up top," he said, gesturing to Sam. Or, more accurately, to her long legs, clearly visible beneath a denim mini skirt.

I shot Derek a warning look.

He gave back an innocent stare in response, then walked over to Julio, watching the child play some alien-sounding game.

Skin folds formed between Sam's perfectly arched brows. "I hope you don't mind. I have no other choices, and I want to make headway with the Peters case. Your dad said it was okay."

I cringed at the word "dad" and walked to her. I pulled her in for a quick hug, spotting the tension and worry in her clenched jaw. "It's fine."

I glanced at the guys. Derek seemed enthralled in the game. Maybe Julio could keep him occupied all day.

I lowered my voice. "In fact, you probably just saved my ass."

* * *

After a morning of literally staring at paint dry (I'd found a bottle of red nail polish in the bathroom cabinet) and listening to the guys squeal as they fought whatever creature-slash-bad guy, I was ready to commit myself. Nothing seemed to pass the time quickly enough. I'd never been much for naps, and lying in the sun meant being exposed to whomever sailed by. Not conducive for hiding out.

I stepped into the galley and found Derek and Julio at the table. Playing cards were spread out between them—a King of hearts, eight and five of diamonds, and a four of spades. The old man was teaching him poker. A mound of yellow, pink, blue, purple, and green cereal nuggets sat to the side.

They stared one another down, as if ready to count six paces then draw their weapons.

Derek laid down his two cards. A King of clubs and four of hearts. "Two pairs, kid. Beat that."

Julio pulled his bottom lip in with his teeth then put down a seven and six of clubs. A wicked smile broke out across his face. "If you insist."

A straight.

I chuckled so loud, I startled myself.

Derek face palmed and groaned into his hand.

Julio giggled, making hissing sounds with his tongue between his front teeth.

"Beginner's luck," Derek said with a smirk. He gathered the cards. "Go get some sunshine. In a bit, I'll teach you Blackjack."

Julio scrambled to his feet, snatched his PSP and ran out.

"Stay away from the edge," I shouted then took his seat. "You think Sam will appreciate you turning her son into a gambler?"

"Ah, he'll have a snazzier 'how I spent my summer vacation' report."

"Yeah, playing poker on a yacht with an old man and a murder suspect. That should go over well with the school district."

I stared out the window, tapping my phone's stylus onto the Formica tabletop. "You're good with him."

Derek grinned. "What can I say? We're on the same wavelength."

A laugh blasted from my throat. "Good point."

"He's a good kid," Derek said, shuffling the deck of cards. "Could use a dad around more, but Sam's doin' okay with him."

"I'm glad you approve," I said, not able to keep the mocking tone from my voice.

And it didn't escape Derek either. He glanced up. "What? You questioning my parenting skills, James?"

I held up my hands. "Who me? Never."

"Hey, we had some good times when you were growin' up," said, dealing us each a hand. "Remember that time I took you to San Diego?"

"On a stake-out," I reminded him.

"And we went to Sea World."

"Following a mark."

"And you got to feed the dolphins."

"While you took pictures of the mark with his girlfriend and her two kids."

Derek grinned at me. "Good times, right?"

I shook my head. While he'd never win father of the year, it was almost as hard to hate Derek as it was to love him.

"You got a phenomenal memory, by the way, James," Derek said, picking up his cards and studying them. "I forgot how many kids she had."

I picked up my cards. I had nothing. "A boy and a girl, both had brown hair, freckles, and the boy was two years older. The girl got a stuffed octopus, and the boy got a toy pirate sword."

Derek glanced at me over the rim of his cards. "See, you're a natural born investigator, James."

Whether it was nature or nurture (or lack thereof), I wasn't sure. But I took the compliment all the same.

"Have you heard from any of your girls?" Derek asked, his eyes going to my right hand. I looked down and realized I was still tapping at the table top.

I forced my hand to be still. "No."

Maya was checking into Club Dante's Shooting Stars trade today, gathering all the info she could on who was using, who was dealing, and where they got their supplies. Sam and Caleigh were, as Sam had stated, working Peters again. They'd protested when I'd said it was business as usual as far as our clients were concerned, but honestly, there wasn't anything else for them to pursue. We were hanging on by a thread as far as leads went, and Club Dante was about it.

And Danny was silent. Not that I expected much from him after I'd told him to take a hike, but part of me kind of wished he'd at least call and make sure Aiden hadn't nabbed me last night.

I loathed to admit Danny had total I-told-you-so-rights. Aiden had played me big time. The easy smile, the warm eyes - I'd bought it all. Even enjoyed it a little, if I was being brutally honest. And all along it had been just to gain info before he threw me in jail. Interrogation 101 - tell your mark what they want to hear, and they'll tell you everything. It had been a long time since I'd let a guy take advantage of me, and I wasn't proud of it. One reason I wasn't entirely unhappy I hadn't heard from Danny today.

Derek placed his cards on the table, face down, apparently folding, and stood. "I better get up there and keep an eye on him. I'm not the strong swimmer I once was."

I nodded, honestly a little touched at his paternal-ness.

But he hesitated in the door, his eyes frowning, mouth working through a few different thoughts before settling on one.

"It's gonna be okay, kid," he finally settled on. "You're tough. You'll get through this."

It was the closest he would ever come to warm and fuzzy. I felt tears back up in my throat, but quickly shoved them down.

"Thanks, Dad."

* * *

After several more butt-numbing hours of card games (I totally won a round of Go Fish.) and listening to the alien sounds from the PSP, I was going insane. I was honestly tempted to raid Derek's liquor cabinet, but instead opted for a box of mac-n-cheese, splitting it with Julio. As I placed a bowl in front of him, his eyes lit up, he shoved a spoonful into his mouth, and the video game was blissfully silent for the first time all day. God bless Kraft.

We were halfway through our bowls of decadent, gooey cheesiness (which, honestly, was making me feel better) when footsteps sounded above us. Two pairs, but I didn't panic this time. They were obviously high heels, and the last time I checked, police officers didn't wear stilettos.

Sam and Caleigh stepped into the gallery.

Julio ran to his mother, wrapping his arms around her waist. "Derek taught me how to play poker, and I won."

She looked to me, brows raised. "Well isn't that sweet of him."

I shrugged. Hey, what do you expect when you chose Derek Bond as your babysitter?

Caleigh snickered and walked over. A black dress was draped over her arm, and a tote bag dangled from her hand.

"How'd it go with Peters today?" I asked.

"Julio, go finish your food," Sam said, automatically. Julio frowned, clearly getting the kids-out-of-the-room signal.

I stood and huddled with them near the sink.

Caleigh's eyes sparkled, and a small smile etched onto her face. "He's not cheating on his wife."

"You're sure?" I asked, hearing my voice drop with disappointment before I could catch it. No cheating equaled no big payday.

They nodded in unison.

"He spent the whole day running errands, playing golf—just all over town." Caleigh rolled her eyes as if thinking about it exhausted her. "And none of it involved a woman."

"But..." Sam teased. She glanced at Julio before whispering, "At one point we lost him, and when we drove past his house we saw Mrs. Peters driving off with another man."

I raised an eyebrow. "Oh reeeally?"

"So I stayed with her while Sam located the husband," Caleigh said, taking turns ping-ponging the information at me.

"Mr. Peters met some guy at Dugan's Tavern for a drink. They laughed, ate way too many peanuts and watched sports," Sam said.

"While Mrs. Peters met some guy at Motel Six, where they played sports for two hours. I don't think peanuts were involved." Caleigh winked.

Part of me was elated to find a husband who believed in his vows. The wife, however, left a bitter taste in my mouth. Why couldn't people simply keep it in their pants until they had nice, civilized divorce papers signed?

"You think she was a kettle calling a pot black?" Sam asked.

I shrugged, trying to remember my first meeting with Mrs. Peters. "More like hoping, I'd guess. She mentioned a prenup. Maybe she wanted to catch him before he caught her."

"We left the video at the office," said Sam. she paused. "The cops finally cleared it."

I nodded, ignoring the reference to my fugitive status. "Perfect. I'll call Mr. Peters on Monday."

"*Mr.* Peters?" Caleigh asked. "I thought our client was the wife."

"She was. But chances are Mr. Peters will pay more than she will to have evidence of his wife's infidelity."

Sam grinned. "You are evil, Jamie."

What I was was broke. But I let the comment go.

"We set for tonight?" I asked.

Caleigh nodded, then handed me a stack of papers. "Maya's research on Shooting Stars."

I glanced down. It was thorough, I'd give her that. "You're ready to run point?" I asked Caleigh.

She nodded.

"What do you want me to do?" Sam asked.

"Go home."

She opened her mouth to protest, a frown forming between her brows again, but I ran over her.

"Julio's had enough of Derek today. Unless you want him turning into a card shark before fifth grade, take him home."

She bit her lower lip. "I could possibly ask my neighbor to watch him again," she offered.

I shook my head. "No, spend time with your son. Caleigh and I got this."

"Yes we do." Caleigh held up the dress. "You'll be wearing this and...."

I grabbed the slinky, low cut garment while she opened the tote.

"These."

She held up a pair of strappy stilettos and an auburn wig.

I always wondered what I'd look like as a redhead.

CHAPTER FOURTEEN

———

Club Dante fit perfectly into the typical L.A. scene: loud music, young bodies, and quickly poured liquor. A triple score. The bigger the thirst, the more they drank, the drunker they became, and the more they talked. My kind of place.

The left wall consisted of the bar, a long lit strip of metal and acrylic. The club's name hung behind it in neon blue and white lights. Three bartenders in fitted blue tees and black pants served the patrons.

Caleigh pushed past a couple hot-glued to one another. The guy's tongue was jammed so far down the petite girl's throat, I thought I saw her eyes roll to the back of her head.

"Sorry," Caleigh yelled after elbowing him in the ribs.

Neither of them flinched or even registered it.

I followed my girl but stayed a few steps behind, observing tonight's crowd. The dance floor throbbed with glistening flesh, in beat to the music and pulsating lights. Wild and carefree, women and men threw up their arms, whipped their hair and gyrated in tempo. It was like watching an African tribal dance, mesmerizing and wicked.

Caleigh pressed against the bar, sending a flirtatious look toward the bartender.

Over six-feet tall, broad shoulders, and hair so blonde it appeared white, he took the time to stop pouring and give her his full attention, despite the line of empty glasses. He could've been on the cover of Sweden's *Sports Illustrated*.

Caleigh batted her thick, false lashes. Her pink tongue darted out, licking cherry lip gloss. And then for the kill, she gave a slow, super flirty smile that made men weak in the zipper.

Another bartender, shorter, darker, but just as buff, threw a towel at Sweden. It cocked him in the ear and fell onto a tray of bar glasses.

Sweden's cheeks reddened. He averted his gaze and went to making a dry martini and cosmopolitan.

A couple to my right stood and walked to the dance floor. Caleigh and I took their seats and raised our glasses.

"To finding the truth and setting you free," she said.

"Yes. And to more days working together at the agency, tracking down cheaters."

She didn't comment, had no idea of Bond's financial situation, and I planned to continue in that mode. At least here's hoping. We clinked and drank.

After a refreshing sip, I turned back to the crowd, calculating who would get us closer to Shooting Stars.

The club scene wasn't much different than high school. You had the guys who tried too hard with their lame pick-up lines, who expected to score, and grew offended or angry when a pretty girl turned them down. The players did score. A lot. The promiscuous girls giggled too loud and drank too much. And the nice ones, the ones who laughed at the lame jokes and left their drinks unattended at the bar, probably weren't regulars. Or wouldn't be for long.

The popular guys and gals appeared to be friends with everyone, kissing cheeks, buying rounds. They attracted the most attention, and rightfully so with their designer cars, attire, and accessories. That IT crowd was who we needed to latch onto tonight. That's where the pills flowed freely, at least according to Maya's research.

A tall, lanky guy rubbed his arm against mine as he reached for his beer on the bar. He grinned at me and quickly averted his eyes. Wearing black trousers, a light blue button-down shirt and tie, he looked ready for the boardroom rather than a night of reckless dancing and hooking up. He'd used too much gel on his drab brown hair, forming a pencil-sharp, top peak.

"Hi. Nice… um, music. It has a great beat, don't you think?"

"Yes." I smiled at his nervousness.

He stared at my cleavage. I was used to men ogling, but he didn't seem the type for such directness.

Caleigh leaned forward and pointed to my brows. "Hey, her eyes are up here."

He turned the hue of beets then walked away.

And sometimes there were the socially awkward.

I shook my head at Caleigh. "You didn't need to embarrass him."

She waved a hand. "Posh, he needs to learn some manners. He can't drool on every beautiful women's tatas."

I chuckled and turned back to categorizing the crowd. A young, well-dressed couple entered and instead of hitting the bar or dance floor, they walked up a semi-spiral staircase at the far end of the room. At the top, they disappeared behind a black-draped wall.

I nodded in that direction. "What's up there?"

"VIP section."

"What makes someone a VIP?"

Caleigh hooked a finger and called Sweden over. They leaned toward one another. She practically straddled the bar and whispered in his ear.

When they parted, she returned to her lady-like, one leg crossed over the other, position. "Basically, if you're a no name, you have to be invited."

I eyed the swaying and sweating mob. So I needed to get close to one of them. No problem. But which one?

I downed the rest of my drink and jumped off the stool. The sudden movement made the room spin in a good way. I grabbed Caleigh's hand.

"Come on. Let's dance."

What better way to garner attention than to make a spectacle of yourself? All the famous, no talent celebs had done it.

We slithered onto the floor, grinding our hips to the bass. The music and vodka weaved through me, creating a spell that transformed me from an impatient PI-slash-homicide-suspect into a music video dancer, bouncing more T&A than Beyonce.

A man straight from the 1970s, with skintight pants, a shirt open to his navel and a thick silver chain, approached. He tried swaying between Caleigh and me, but we stepped closer. There was no way I'd allow a *Saturday Night Live* reject touch us.

Caleigh slung her arm around my waist and nuzzled her ear against my cheek. Several heads turned. Luckily Mr. Suave-Not disappeared.

A couple of other guys stepped closer though. The one by my side smelled like money and looked like an Armani ad. He was probably my age, if not a bit younger. He roved my body, and a cocky smile tugged one side of his mouth.

"Are you two together, or were you just trying to get away from that creep?" he shouted into my ear.

"Creep."

He nodded, and his smile widened.

The other man wasn't as polished, but a light smattering of freckles across the bridge of his nose and the tops of his cheeks made him endearing. He and Caleigh began bumping and grinding.

Which left me with... "What's your name?"

"Garret. Sumners."

I knew the name. Sumners, as in, son of Dolores Sumners, major Hollywood actress and someone who could get me upstairs?

"Jamie Cartier."

What? It was the first thing that came to mind.

If I hadn't been intentionally looking for his reaction, I might've missed the slight quirk of his brows, especially under the throbbing lights.

"I haven't seen you here before."

"I just flew in from New York this afternoon. Contemplating moving here."

"So you check out the nightlife right away?"

"Absolutely. I don't know if it can compare to the five boroughs though."

He held out his arms. "Is this too shabby for you?" Laughter laced his voice.

"I've heard L.A. has some super sweet amp. Like watching Shooting Stars," I fished.

"Oh yeah? You're into that?"

I shrugged. "Is that a bad thing?"

He shook his head, his eyes full of lust. "Not at all. I may know where you can get something that'll have you purring like a kitten."

I trailed a fingernail down his chest, over the ripples of his six-pack. "I also roar and pounce."

Chatting in the middle of a club wasn't easy. Still, his chuckle was smooth, almost electric, and chased away some of my anxiety.

There was something different about him. He didn't drool or have roving eyes. At least not that much. Sure, he was flirting, but it was on a different level. One that said he was confident the night would end the way he wanted it to.

He leaned closer until his long bangs fell forward and caressed the side of my face. I could smell his coconut shampoo. "I'll have to prove L.A. is more thrilling than New York."

A challenge. I giggled and fluttered my lashes. "You're on."

We fell into rhythm and danced. My body buzzed with excitement. My gut screamed he was my ticket upstairs and getting closer to the truth.

Then a couple of scantily clad young women pushed their way through the crowd, over to us.

My stomach cramped. This was not going to be good. They were younger, sluttier, and looked like regulars. I hated competition.

The blonder of the two poked Caleigh's dance partner in the back. When he turned around, she raised her arm and slapped him, open palm across the cheek.

He flinched from the attack.

She smacked the freckled guy's arm and stomped off. He followed, shoulders slumped.

The other girl, orange-complexioned from way too much tanning, cupped Garret's bicep. He nodded in her direction but didn't stop dancing. Obviously not a romantic couple.

One point in my favor. I shimmied a little closer to my prey.

The orange girl glared at me. Clearly she thought I was invading her territory.

She yelled, "Who's she?"

Garret winked at me then said, "A new friend. She'll be hanging with us tonight."

Score one point for my low-cut dress.

Orange scoffed. "Over my dead body, Garret."

"That can be arranged," I shouted, sending her a sugary sweet smile.

Garret roared with laughter. If only either of them knew I was already on the police's top ten list. He turned and said something to the pumpkin that made the corners of her mouth downturn, but the glare remained.

"Who's the mean girl?" Caleigh asked, not caring who heard. It was part of her charm.

Garret faced us and said, "This is my sister, Chloe."

I wasn't easily shocked, but that did it. The way she looked at him was possessive, but that was not the relationship I'd envisioned.

"Who are you?" Chloe yelled at me.

Garret started to introduce me when Caleigh jumped in and said, "She's Jamie. Her father invented *Toaster Scrambles*."

The connection to the *Mean Girls* movie never registered in Chole's eyes, but Garret caught on and pressed his lips together, forming a thin line.

"Come on," he said and led us off the dance floor.

Caleigh and I followed the siblings upstairs. With each step, my skin tingled with anticipation. Up top, we entered a lounge. Long, sleek sofas outlined the room, a few high tables and stools took up the center space. There was no door, yet the area wasn't as loud as below. Now we could have a real conversation, and I wouldn't sound like Kermit the Frog in the morning.

There were a handful of young, attractive bodies drinking, talking, making out. Heads turned as we strode across the soft, black carpet, but only momentarily. Showing interest was so not-chic.

Garret nodded a greeting to each of the patrons, then motioned to a waitress, requesting a bottle of champagne. He sat on the sofa along the back wall then patted the seat beside him.

I sank into the plush suede.

Garret leaned into me. "My connection should be here soon."

My heartbeat thundered. This could be a step closer to the truth or down a dead-end street. Again.

Caleigh sat at one of the tables with a man twice her age. The older ones always found her alluring. Something about her Southern gentility.

Chloe sat on the other side of Garret, practically stitched to his hip. She'd make a great Siamese twin.

Several people came and went. I spotted joints, ecstasy, and Oxy, but nothing I didn't know of or recognize.

Chloe and Garret began bickering in hushed tones. I looked away but tried to zero in on their words. Unfortunately some guy to my left shouted to his date, making my eavesdropping null and void.

I turned as the latest arrivals entered. A muscular, dark-haired guy that looked about seventeen, and a leggy woman with an adorable jet black bob and straight bangs.

She glanced to the siblings, and I noticed her infamous icy grey eyes and the heart-shaped beauty mark at the left side of her mouth.

I knew her. Not personally, more like *of* her. I raised a brow at Caleigh who must've recognized her as well. The young woman was Dakota Hall, an up and coming model for DeLine. I may have been out of the runway game, but I still kept tabs on the newbies.

"I can't believe she's here," Chloe whispered after waving to Dakota.

Garret nodded. His expression grew sullen.

"Why?" I asked.

"You'd think she'd at least pretend to care about a death in the family. At least for the press's sake," Chloe scoffed.

"A death?" I asked, feeling my spidey-senses tingle.

Garret nodded. "Her uncle was just murdered. It's been big news here."

The earth opened, and I teetered on the edge, staring down into its lava-filled center.

"Who was her uncle?" My voice cracked. I already knew the answer, but I felt my stomach flip as he said the words anyway.

"Judge Thomas Waterston."

CHAPTER FIFTEEN

———

I watched Dakota sashay around the room, air-kiss everyone, and settle on the sofas to my right, my heart thudding double time in my chest. She gave me a tight lipped greeting, as if she wasn't sure if I was friend or foe.

I returned the expression, but in a more charming, albeit fake fashion. Then I looked away and pretended interest in the conversation to my left. Something to do with sushi restaurants and the level of mercury in fish.

Riveting.

Garret and Chloe stood. Their arguing had continued while Dakota had made her rounds. To me, he said, "I'll be right back," then they disappeared downstairs.

Which I took as my opening. Dakota being here wasn't coincidence, whether I believed in it or not. Too many people were connected to this club, and it was time to find out just how.

The guy with Dakota whispered in her ear. She rolled her eyes and shook her head. He leaned closer, and she pulled back ever so slightly. She looked away, and I did the same, not wanting to get caught staring.

As a DeLine model, was it possible she'd recognize me? In the Hall of Fame, AKA the long corridor that led to Maurcess DeLine's office, a poster of me hung. I wore a pair of booty shorts and half-top, and I was covered in mud. Reminiscent of Daisy Dukes but with less sass and more couture.

All best photos of top models resided in the hall. Dakota had to pass it whenever she visited DeLine. I used to study the poses of the models that had succeeded before me.

Dakota scowled, and her guy frowned. It was like watching a couple of children. He stood up and stomped across the room.

She scooted over into his spot, clearly telling him not to return, and I honed in on the opportunity.

I popped up, then sat down beside her. With an exasperated air, I sighed and bobbed my head toward the deep sea lovers. "Ugh, they're talking about tuna, and I'm so allergic."

She glanced from me to them and back again. A frown puckered the space between her thinly waxed brows. She was trying to place me, I could tell. I prayed the auburn wig did its job. "They say it's so good for you," she finally agreed, "but it smells awful."

"No kidding!" I petted her fuzzy, leopard purse. "This is gorgeous. Where'd you get it?"

Her eyes lit up. She was a fashion girl, clearly. "It was a gift from a special guy."

"The one who just left?"

She scrunched up her face. "God, no. He's a tool."

"Kind of a cute tool, though." I giggled like a schoolgirl and almost rolled my eyes at the obnoxious sound.

"Yeah, but he tries to boss me around, and I don't need a father."

"Oh my God, I know exactly what you mean. Why do some guys get pushy?"

She turned her body toward me, her rose perfume engulfing me.

I gagged and played it off as a cough, sipping my champagne and breathing through my mouth.

"I know, right?" she said. "They think they own you. What's with that?"

"It's not like they pay our bills."

"Exactly. I don't need a sugar daddy. I make my own money. And anything I can't afford, I have a very generous uncle."

A breath trapped in my lungs.

The shift of her eyes suggested she remembered he was currently residing six-feet under and no longer writing checks.

Before the mood darkened, I yelled, "Plus, aren't you like famous? I've seen you on magazine covers."

The haunted mask vanished, and she beamed again. "Yes. I'm a model. Dakota Hall." She held out her petite hand.

I placed my fingers against hers and gave one of those girly handshakes. The kind that suggests I have no power; I'm not a threat.

"I'm Jamie Cartier. New in town. Garret Sumners invited me up here."

She cooed. "Oh my God, Garret is yummy, right?"

"Yes, he is."

The waitress arrived with a round of drinks for the room, paid for by Fish Boy. We all nodded our thanks, cheered to his generosity, and then Dakota and I settled back into the cushions.

"It's not like he and I would last anyway," Dakota said, jumping back into conversation so quickly I took a moment to realize who she was talking about.

"The tool?"

She nodded. "He's twenty-two and still doesn't know what he wants to do with his life. Can you imagine?"

In other parts of the world, guys that age either graduated college and moved back home while looking for a job or had never left to begin with. But not in Hollywood. You were considered a loser if you weren't on a clear path to stardom by the ripe age of sixteen.

"That's absurd." I may have laid the sarcasm on a little thick, but she hadn't noticed.

"What about you? Do you have a special guy?"

I frowned and shook my head. "No. All the guys I know are either childishly protective or lying assholes." Not that I was thinking of any two guys in particular.

Her head bobbed up and down in agreement.

We spent the next half hour chit-chatting about men. She gave me tips on how to model, as if, and pretended she wasn't aware of her guy flirting with every girl in the room, including Caleigh.

I tried to steer the conversation to her personal life, but she didn't give out many details, and she was tight lipped about her uncle. It wasn't like I could blatantly ask.

The tool grabbed some girl's butt, watching Dakota the entire time. The girl squealed, and Dakota scoffed. "Hey, you wanna get out of here?" she asked me.

My heartbeat accelerated. "Sure."

But instead of the two of us leaving alone, she invited half the room. A party at Dakota Hall's place.

Garret hadn't returned, and unless someone at the party carried Shooting Stars that part of the night was a bust. But I figured Dakota was too good a lead to drop. While I had a hard time picturing the party girl as a mastermind behind a complicated murder and frame-up, she was clearly the link between Donna Martinez and the judge. Had she and Donna been friends? Had she introduced Donna to the killer? Had the killer been a friend of the both of them? One of the IT crowd currently surrounding us? I prayed I was about to find out.

As we stood to leave, I caught Caleigh's eye. She hadn't been invited, and for me to suggest she come may have aroused suspicion.

I gave her an I'll-be-fine stare and hurried out to Dakota's waiting limo.

* * *

Dakota spent the entire ride on the phone in some hushed conversation. Instead of sitting beside her, I sat squished between a loud guy in skinny jeans and his date, a tiny girl who giggled nonstop. I wasn't able to hear any of Dakota's conversation.

Her apartment turned out to be a penthouse. We stepped off the private elevator, and I nearly gasped. It wasn't as large as I imagined, but I could tell that the place had set her uncle back mega bucks. There was no way she afforded this on her own.

A gas fireplace snuggled against the back wall beside the L-shaped stairs, opposite the elevator. The other two walls consisted of glass, floor-to-ceiling windows. To say the view was breathtaking was an understatement.

Everyone pushed through the doors, settling onto her leather furniture, turning on the stereo, lighting a fire, despite the blowing A/C. She must have had these impromptu gatherings often. They all fell into a groove, as if each person had their own task.

I made my way to the windows beside the stairs, calculating how long before I could slip away and investigate upstairs.

Dakota and another woman emerged from a side room with several bottles of champagne. Corks popped, and someone handed me a glass of champagne before making a toast.

I joined them in the center of the living room.

"To Dakota, the best supermodel DeLine has ever known."

Everyone cheered. I bit my tongue.

The elevator doors opened and Garret and Chloe stepped into the room. I felt a lift of hope grab at my stomach. Maybe my Shooting Stars connection wasn't a colossal bust after all.

Garret did a quick survey of the room, immediately meeting my eyes. He patted his jacket pocket and winked.

Bingo.

This night just kept getting better.

My heels clicked across Dakota's hardwood floors as I quickly cozied up to my "supplier", despite Chloe's scowl.

"Where's your friend?" he asked me.

"She couldn't make it."

"I'm glad *you* did."

I caught my delighted reflection in his eyes. "Me too."

Chloe dramatically yawned then walked over to Skinny Jeans.

"She doesn't seem to like me," I pointed out, as soon as she was out of earshot.

Garret shrugged. "We've been close our whole lives. I've helped her out of a lot of jams. She feels she needs to look out for my best interests, too."

"And clearly she doesn't see me as in your best interests."

He grinned. "I'm sure once she gets to know you, she'll have a change of heart."

I glanced her way. Although she talked to Skinny Jeans, she was still shooting daggers my way.

I felt like telling her not to worry. Beyond tonight, I had no use for either of the Club Kid siblings.

I grabbed Garret's arm, ignoring looks from his sister, and followed him into the center of the room where he nabbed a glass of champagne. Then he pulled me down next to him on one of the gleaming white sofas and reached into his jacket pocket.

"Here." He held out his hand and dropped two nondescript, white pills into my palm. "Only one at a time."

"They'll send me to the moon?" I asked, turning them over.
"All the way and back."

"Thanks. I hope they weren't hard for you to get."

He popped one into his mouth and swallowed it dry. "Not at all. You just need the right connections."

I raised my hand to my mouth and pretended to take a pill. I sipped from my glass, tossed my head back for affect, and dropped both pills into my clutch.

"You know, I was a little worried when you disappeared earlier," I told him. "I wasn't sure you were coming back."

He grinned at me. "Baby, I wouldn't pass up an opportunity like this." His hand went around my shoulders, his fingers squeezing suggestively at my bare arm.

I looked up at him through my eyelashes. "I'm glad you weren't gone long. Your connection was nearby?"

He nodded. "I got connections all over. Don't you worry. Anything you want, I can get."

Scary. But I was interested in just one connection in particular tonight.

"I got the feeling your connection was at the club," I hinted coyly.

Garret just smiled, his eyes lazy as he watched me.

"Don't tell me... it's that bartender with the spiked hair, right?" I fished, watching him for any indication I was on the right track.

But he just grinned wider. I couldn't tell if it was the drugs taking effect already or if he thought he was being seductive.

I was trying to phrase my next question, when Skinny Jeans hailed Garret from the other side of the room. My "date" turned his lazy gaze toward his friend, excusing himself as he got up.

As frustrated as I was at not getting a name out of him, I recognized an opportunity to slip upstairs when I saw one.

I mumbled, "Restroom," to anyone who might have been within earshot and quickly made my way up the marble tiled staircase.

A hallway led off the landing in two directions. To the right, I spied a guest bathroom, to the left a series of what looked like bedrooms.

I passed a guest room, neat, professionally decorated, and unused looking. Another followed, similarly outfitted with brass furniture and floral bedding that clearly spoke to an older decorating hand than Dakota's. I passed by, going for a set of closed double doors at the end of the hallway. I slowly grabbed the handles and pushed one down.

It opened, and a hint of rose petals greeted me. I paused, listening for sounds within. I had tried to keep tabs on everyone at the party, but I couldn't be certain someone hadn't slipped up here for a little private time. Luckily, only my own breath greeted my ears. I slipped inside, quickly shutting the doors behind me.

A small bedside lamp cast a soft glow over the room. A large, pink-clad bed took up one side of the room, an array of cocktail dresses cast off on its surface. Shoes, handbags, an assortment of cosmetics littered the rest of the room, the mess clashing with the custom furnishings in dark woods with gleaming silver fittings. A huge portrait of Dakota in a bikini hung above the bed. Tacky.

I raided the dresser first, opening the top drawer, looking for anything that might point toward the girl's guilt. I pushed around panties, bras, tee shirts, camisoles, teddys, pjs, shorts. But the only thing I learned was that Dakaota's lingerie tended toward the slutty, and she had a distinct favoritism toward leopard prints.

I was just moving on to the closet when I heard footsteps echo in the hallway outside the door.

I froze.

"Dakota?" I heard a voice call.

It was Skinny Jeans. I quickly tiptoed to the closet, stepping into a walk-in larger than my entire office, and closed the door behind me. I backed into the corner, slowly, held my breath and stepped on several pairs of pumps. The heels knocked together, sounding explosive to my super-hyped ears.

The bedroom door opened. "Dakota?" the guy called. "You in here?"

I held my breath.

Footsteps moved into the room, making a slow circle. Finally they paused, then retreated back the way they'd come, shutting the bedroom door behind them.

I waited a beat, forcing my breathing to return to normal. It was only a matter of minutes before someone noticed I was missing and came looking again.

I opened the doors, doing a quick scan of the closet, before deciding it held nothing more incriminating than an array of slutty clothes at designer prices.

Feeling borrowed time tick by, I flew around the room like a whirlwind, checking the nightstands and under the bed - looking for anything that said Dakota might have been the one to hire Donna. Or that she knew who did.

I spun through the master bath, quickly going through medicine cabinets and countless make-up drawers. While Dakota had an impressive number of prescriptions for such a seemingly young and healthy girl, none matched the pills Garret had given me.

I was running out of places to look.

I scanned the room, a black bookcase along the back wall the only place I'd yet to tear apart. Rather than holding a library of actual books, there were dozens of framed photos arranged on the shelves, most of them holding pictures of Dakota in various poses. I took a step toward it, grabbing a black, leather-bound book from the top shelf. I flipped it open, greeted by an eight-by-ten glossy of Dakota on a beach. Her modeling portfolio.

While I knew there was nothing here that related to her uncle's death, I couldn't help idle curiosity getting the better of me. I thumbed through a few pages, seeing photos of her in evening gowns, contorting into ridiculous poses that I knew only too well. There were quite a few bikini shots, a couple that I recognized as having been shot in Malibu. And one, I noticed, honing in on a photo halfway through the book, that looked eerily familiar. Dakota was posed on a cropping of jagged rocks, overlooking the Pacific, her eyes looking out to sea, her body curled protectively over itself in an artful way that somehow still looked graceful. I knew this location. And I knew that pose. It was the same one I'd been instructed to take by my photographer years ago.

With my heart thudding wildly in my chest, I flipped the page over, checking the photographer's imprint on the back.

And almost dropped the book when I read it.

Daniel Flynn.

CHAPTER SIXTEEN

———

Time stood still as I stared at the imprinted name, my mind racing.

Okay, so Danny had photographed her. He'd photographed lots of girls. DeLine used him all the time. It stood to reason that Dakota had spent some time in front of his camera.

What didn't stand to reason was that Danny hadn't mentioned it. I'd been searching for a link between Donna Martinez and the judge, but staring me in the face was an even more important link. One between the judge and *me*. Why had I specifically been picked to be the scapegoat to his murder? Was it coincidence that one of my closest friends knew the niece of the guy I was accused of killing?

But even as I mentally chewed on that thought, I knew the answer. I'd never believed in coincidence before, and now was a lousy time to start.

Danny purposely hadn't mentioned her. Why?

The book trembled in my unsteady hands. Anxiety, anger and betrayal washed over me all at once in a muddy swirl.

Danny had wanted me to hire an attorney. He'd urged me to turn myself in. He'd gotten angry when I'd said Aiden believed me, that I was meeting with him. At the time, I'd thought it was some over-protective, macho gesture. But what if the hide he'd been protecting was not mine but his own?

I'd known Danny for years. Even as I saw evidence of his lie staring me in the face, I had a hard time believing he would deliberately set me up to take the fall for murder.

But he was definitely involved. And definitely hiding something.

I flipped through the pages of the book, checking imprints on the back now, not the actual images. At least a dozen bore Danny's name. I felt sicker with each one, my stomach rolling on itself. I shut the book, shoved it back on the shelf.

Just as the bedroom door opened, and Dakota stepped inside.

Shit.

Her eyes widened, then she frowned. "What are you doing in here?"

I blinked, not prepared for an interrogation, my mind still racing with the million WTF's the portfolio had inspired.

"Well?" she asked again, shutting the door behind her.

I clutched my stomach, knowing damn well I appeared shaken and about to lose it. "I wasn't feeling well and was looking for a restroom. The other one was full," I lamely explained.

She stared at me for a long minute then scrunched her nose up. "Well, if you're gonna be sick, please don't do it in here. Like, go use the kitchen sink or something."

I nodded. "Right. Sorry." Then I practically sprinted out of the room without hesitation. When she closed the door behind me, I figured it was the perfect time to make my escape. I slipped down the staircase, quickly grabbed my purse from the sofa, and slipped out the door before anyone even noticed I was gone.

* * *

A cab dropped me off back at the club where I grabbed my car and immediately drove toward the office. It was a risk, but I needed answers, and this was the only place to get them.

I moved slowly, first checking the street for unassuming cars that looked like detectives in cheap suits lived in them, then scanning the building for any sign of new surveillance cameras. All looked clear. And eerily quiet.

I made my way down the hall in the dark. No sense in attracting any possible attention from outside. I hit my office, then I pulled my blinds shut tight and flipped on the lamp beside my computer.

My leather chair embraced me like an old pair of jeans, worn and comfortable in all the right places. I closed my eyes and listened to the silence, needing a moment to recoup.

I switched on my computer while mentally replaying every conversation Danny and I'd had in the past week. Funny how one little piece of information could put an entirely different spin on everything he'd said to me.

While I typed Dakota's name into a search engine, I wondered if Danny had really betrayed me for the leggy model. It wouldn't be the first time he'd done something stupid over a woman. I hadn't pegged Dakota as the brains behind the murder plot, but it's certainly possible she was a better actress than I gave her credit for.

Links to Dakota's website, *Facebook* and *Twitter* accounts popped up on my screen. Several articles showed her photo shoots in *Seventeen* and *Glamour;* one looked demure and teen-like while the other was full vamp. An interview listed her favorite movie as *American Pie* and her favorite dessert as apple because it reminded her of the film.

I added Danny's name to the search engine and received several mentions of them together on a photo shoot in Brazil. That was last year.

My stomach rolled again. Had they known each other that long? It gave them an awful lot of time to get cozy. And an awful lot of time for Dakaota to milk Danny for info about yours truly. I wondered how willingly he'd given it.

I browsed a few more pages, picking up little bits and pieces about Dakota that meant nothing on their own, but I filed them away for future info anyway. Then I turned off the computer and grabbed a camera from my bottom desk drawer. An old Nikon that Danny had given me a couple of years back when he was updating his equipment.

I tucked it into my jacket beside my Glock and headed out.

Fifteen minutes later, I was parked across from Danny's apartment, a block down the street. I faced the door, taking a front row seat to any activity to or from the building. It was too early, too dark for him to be awake.

But I could wait.

* * *

A horn honked, and I jumped. I rubbed my eyes, smearing day-old mascara and eyeliner.

It was daylight, dawn. The sky was a pale grey, but the sun hadn't risen yet. I blinked into the hazy morning.

The horn blasted again, and I turned to glare. A car sat perpendicular to mine, only a couple of feet away. The windows were down, and a woman yelled obscenities at the car in front of her, which was idle at the stop sign.

She gripped her cell phone in one hand and a coffee in the other. The older man in the front car flipped up his middle finger then sped around the corner.

Good morning, L.A.

Miss Obscenities drove on using the tips of her fingers to steer. She never even noticed me.

I grabbed my cell off the passenger seat. Six o'clock. I stretched, as best as possible behind a steering wheel, and considered driving down the block to get a cup of coffee. But I didn't want to miss Danny leave. He'd be up and out soon.

I grabbed the camera and took a few shots of the front of his building. Then waited. My stomach rumbled, and I fished through the glove compartment for a piece of gum, a leftover fortune cookie, anything. But all I found were ketchup packets, napkins and a book of matches.

For a brief moment I wondered if heated ketchup would satisfy the hunger.

I played with my phone and discovered two voicemails. I dialed in and listened. The first one was from Derek, wanting a recap of the night. His tone sounded edgy and concerned.

I made a mental note to call him later, then deleted the message and went on to the second.

It was from Caleigh. "You haven't checked in. I'm worried. And when I worry I get those tiny lines between my brows, and you know how I feel about lines. So call me when you get this."

I smiled at her concern, then quickly shot her a text telling her I was okay.

Relatively speaking.

Movement up ahead made me look up. The building door opened, and a pair of tall, athletic blondes bounced out. Danny's neighbors in 4B. He said they were Pilates instructors who had yet to give him the time of day. It hadn't stopped him from repeatedly trying, though.

They walked down the street and out of sight.

I set the camera on my lap, my body humming, ready for action. I took a deep breath and slowly exhaled, trying an old meditation technique I'd learned during my first photo shoot in lingerie. Filming in see-through lace at seventeen hadn't sounded like a nerve-wracking idea until I got onto the set and saw all the cameras and people gawking. Luckily, one of the makeup artists taught me how to tune everyone else out through relaxation.

I continued the breaths until my pulse calmed.

Just as the door opened, and Danny stepped outside.

I lifted the camera and took a couple of shots.

He blinked at the sky and shielded his eyes with his hand, as if sunlight blinded him. Knowing him, he'd just climbed out of bed and hadn't pulled up a shade yet.

I continued to watch him through the lens.

He was top and shoeless, only wearing grey sweats and a smile. What was he grinning at? He glanced back at the door.

It opened further, and out stepped Dakota, still dressed in the black linen shorts and nude colored halter she'd worn at the club.

Her appearance sucker punched me in the gut, and all those relaxing deep breaths gushed out my window.

"Son of a bitch."

Dakota reached up on tippy-toes and planted a firm kiss on Danny's mouth.

The "special guy" who'd bought her the purse I'd admired at the club. The hushed conversation with someone in the limo. It had been Danny. Had she been telling him about me? Warning him that I was getting close?

I jabbed and released the camera's button continuously. The shutter opened and closed in rapid speed, echoing like distant gun fire.

Danny leaned into the kiss and grabbed Dakota's ass.

She pulled away, giggled and waved as she walked down the road to her car.

He turned and went back inside.

I gripped the edge of the camera until I thought I'd snap it in two.

My best friend was now my prime suspect. I couldn't trust anyone.

I clenched my teeth until I thought the enamel would crack.

God, I hated it when Derek was right.

CHAPTER SEVENTEEN

———

I counted to ten, but blood still pounded in my ears. I'd been duped.

Before I could chicken shit my way out of this confrontation, I tossed my camera onto the passenger seat. I grabbed my keys, hopped out, locked the door and stomped to his building. It's not that I was afraid of confrontations. I got right in the middle of them every time I hunted down a husband. They were usually someone else's mess though.

Palm flat against the blue painted wood, I pushed past the lobby door and walked up two flights of stairs. By the time I reached Danny's floor, my panting matched my heart rate. Fast, uneven and full of anger.

I glared at the gold painted 3C nailed to his door. I didn't bother to knock but turned the knob.

The door swung fast, slammed against the back wall and ricocheted toward me. My heels clicked-clacked across the hardwood floors. I stopped in the middle of the room. "Where are you?" I demanded of the empty space. His place was tiny, small enough to fit neatly inside Dakota's bedroom. But, it was tidy by bachelor standards, the bulk of it being taken up by a tan sofa and a wall of photographic equipment.

Danny poked his head out from the kitchen, confusion lighting his face the second he saw me.

He stepped into the room, an empty coffee pot in hand. "James? What are you doing here?"

"I know," I told him, my words coming loud and fast.

He shrugged and tried to look nonchalant, but the corner of his mouth twitched. "You know what."

"Everything," I bluffed.

"That covers a lot of ground."

"You really want this conversation to go down this way?" I asked him. "After everything we've been through?"

The confusion deepened, though I could see another emotion peeking through. If I had to guess, it looked a lot like guilt. "I don't know what you're talking about, Jamie."

"I'm talking about you screwing a possible murderer. Then screwing me to cover it."

His mouth twitched again. "You're not making any sense."

He was actually going to stand here and try to deny it? Would I need to run downstairs and show him the pictures?

"Why?" I asked. "Just tell me why you did it? Is she really that good in bed?"

His eyes narrowed. "Who are you talking about?"

"Dakota Hall!" I yelled, the name screeching out of me. "I saw her leaving your place, so the denial thing is just a waste of time."

He paused. "So what?"

"*So what*? So you slept with her!"

Danny blinked at me. "Yeah, I did. I didn't realize I needed your permission."

"Christ, Danny," I said, running a hand through my messy wig. "How could you do this to me?"

"Look," he said, taking a step backward. "I don't know what the hell you're talking about. But whatever it is, you gotta simmer down, Bond." He turned his back on me and headed toward the kitchen.

My heart thumped against my rib cage, his suggestion to "simmer down" only having the opposite effect on me. I leapt forward and grabbed Danny's arm, squeezing his bicep, trying to hold him back.

"I'm not done with you yet," I growled.

His eyes darted to mine. Instead of their usual paleness, they reminded me of the Pacific Ocean during low tide, dark, dangerous.

We both knew I couldn't pin him down, but he must've seen the determination in my face because he tossed the coffee pot onto the sofa and wrapped his hand around mine.

His grip crushed my fingers, prying them off one at a time.

I snatched my hand back and slapped his face.

He took a step back, clearly stunned. "What's wrong with you?" he yelled.

"You." I raised my hand and slapped him again, feeling the bubble of hurt and anger welling up in my throat. I hit him again, his arms going up to his face protectively.

"How could you do this to me? Over some dumb bimbo? You'd throw away our entire friendship over some hot little piece of ass."

"Stop!" Danny said, grabbing my right wrist.

But I noticed he didn't deny it, didn't defend himself.

The fingers of my left hand curled into a fist.

"Why would you frame me for murder?"

I punched his bicep.

He grunted and flashed me a look of disbelief, but didn't utter a word. No acknowledgment. No defense. No apology.

"What have I ever done to you?" I asked.

I raised my fist again and aimed for his face. But when I swung, something stopped me.

A large hand engulfed mine, preventing my next attack.

"That's enough," whispered a deep voice.

I froze.

I knew that voice.

I spun around to find myself face to face with Aiden.

I blinked, trying to register his presence here.

"What the hell are *you* doing here?" Danny asked, practically growling his words.

But Aiden didn't answer him, just slowly guided my arm down and around my back.

"Wait, what are you doing?" I asked, even as the slow realization hit me.

A uniformed police officer stepped into view behind Aiden and snapped a handcuff around my wrist.

Aiden let go and stood in front of me. His right eye was swollen and turning a pale shade of purple where I'd caught him the night before.

He withdrew a sheet of paper from his jacket's breast pocket. It looked like an official document, but I didn't concentrate on it.

Instead I glared from him to Danny, not sure which one I hated more.

The officer tugged my other arm around and tightened the cuffs. Then Aiden uttered the words I dreaded most.

"James Bond, we have a warrant for your arrest in the murder of Judge Thomas Waterston."

CHAPTER EIGHTEEN

———

The next thirty hours sped by faster than any of my life. In record time, I'd been booked, arraigned by special order of the ADA, and held without bail. I'd never seen the justice system work this quickly. I supposed a part of me ought to be flattered.

It wasn't until I'd totally lost track of what day it was that I'd been escorted into a room with a metal table and two chairs. I was plunked into one, and a beat later the door opened again, and Aiden sat in the other.

He placed down a beige file, averting his eyes from mine. Wimp. His hair tufted up at the ears and dark crescents hugged his eyes. He looked worse than I did, and I'd spent the night praying for sleep on a mattress thinner than my patience.

This was the first time I'd been alone with him since I was arrested. The cops interrogated me yesterday, along with my public defender—an older man with white hair and beard that resembled Santa. The only time I'd seen Aiden was in the courtroom this morning when a judge, wielding an angry gavel, agreed with him that I was a flight risk and needed to be remanded without bail. Waterston's colleague barely listened to Santa's request for bond. A fair trial wasn't possible.

In addition to the need for a shower, hot latte and something with a lower polyester blend than the fabulous orange jumpsuit I was sporting, I wanted to scream, tear up Aiden's documents, and scratch his eyes out. But I didn't need more evidence of my temper, so I sat still, balling my fists under the table as I watched him avoid me.

"You can't even look me in the eye," I said, making the first move.

His head shot up, his eyes finally meeting mine.

Then quickly looking away again.

"You have to understand that some things are out of my control," he said, his voice way more apologetic than I'd anticipated.

"I am not a flight risk," I told him. "Where would I fly to?"

He blinked and straightened his tie. In a thick voice he said, "I didn't have a choice."

"We all have choices, Aiden. I chose to trust you. You chose to stab me in the back."

He crinkled his brow. "That's not true."

"Ha!" My laugh came out over-the-top and maniacal, kinda matching my mood. "What the hell do you call what happened in the park? The police just happened to show up?"

He paused. "That wasn't me. I didn't call them."

"Then who did?" I asked, not believing him for a second.

"I don't know. They got a tip."

"How convenient," I said, leaning back in my chair.

"I'm not lying to you, Jamie," he insisted.

"Fine," I said, calling his bluff. "Then who sent in the tip?"

"It was anonymous. But the police traced it to a gym in North Hollywood." He looked down at his notes. "Crunches."

I felt heat radiate through my body, making me dizzy and wish for a paper bag. Or a bucket.

That was where Danny worked out. There was that coincidence again.

Aiden leaned forward and lowered his voice. "I haven't lied to you, Jamie. About anything. Every word was the truth."

I wasn't sure if the whispers were so those on the other side of the mirror-like glass couldn't hear his declaration of honesty, or to create a false sense of intimacy before he interrogated me.

"Well this," I said, gesturing around me, "isn't exactly a vote of confidence in me. I thought you said you believed me."

He gave me a long look. "Personal feelings aside, I'm still bound by the law."

Personal feelings? My mind jumped on the word, an image of the cute, flirtatious Aiden I'd met at the fundraiser momentarily flickering across my mind. It seemed like a lifetime ago. I quickly shoved any "personal feelings" I may have had about it aside, focusing on his words as he continued.

"I told you it doesn't matter what I believe," he said. "It matters what I can-"

"Prove," I finished for him. "I know."

He clamped his lips together, looking pained, like he wanted to say more, but his listeners on the other side of the glass prevented it. "I'm sorry."

"Join the club," I mumbled back. I waited as silence hung in the room. Then asked, "Did Danny somehow tell you I was at his place yesterday, too?"

Aiden shook his head. "We had eyes on his apartment."

I nodded. I should have expected that. I was so blinded by my anger at Danny that I wasn't thinking clearly. He was my closest friend - or so I'd thought. Of course the police would be watching his place for me.

"We figured you'd show up eventually," Aiden explained, confirming my suspicions. "From what I could find, you seem close to him."

My stomach tightened. "Seemed."

He cocked his head at the past tense, but didn't ask me to elaborate.

"So what now?" I asked.

Aiden purposely averted his eyes again. "Now I have to ask you some questions."

"Fine." I crossed my arms over my chest. "But I don't have to answer without Sant-" I stopped myself just in time. "My public defender present."

"It would be to your benefit to answer," Aiden informed me.

"I doubt that."

"Jamie, the police found the gun that killed Judge Waterston."

Lead pooled in my stomach, sinking me further into the hard chair.

"And?" I asked, knowing there was an "and" and dreading it with all my heart.

He sighed deeply. "Your fingerprints are on it."

I blinked hard. This wasn't real. I never touched any gun but my own, which had been on my person when they'd arrested me.

"Can you explain that?" Aiden asked, his eyes searching mine as if he truly hoped I could.

I just slowly shook my head back and forth.

Again with the deep sigh. "We found something in your purse," he continued. He pulled a clear baggie out of the file, sliding it across the table to me. In it were the two Shooting Stars Garret had given me.

I closed my eyes and thought a really bad word.

"Where did you get them?" Aiden asked.

I didn't respond.

"I want to help you, Jamie, but you have to trust me."

I opened my eyes. "I'm sorry if trust is a commodity I'm a little short on these days," I shot back.

Aiden's gaze shot through me, the line of his jaw hardening. "Look, this is no game here, Jamie. We potentially have enough evidence to put you away for a very long time. You have to give me something if you want me to help you."

I gave him a long, hard look.

Then told him, "No more questions without my attorney."

* * *

An hour later, back in my cell, I stared up at the chipping paint on the ceiling. Santa had arrived and tried to field Aiden's questions, but even with his presence, I'd refused to answer any of them. Mostly because I didn't *have* answers.

They'd informed me that my preliminary hearing was scheduled for the morning. At this rate, I'd be tried and convicted before my scrumptious dinner of canned beans arrived.

"I know you from somewhere," said my just-arrived roomie, a tall, linebacker-type woman with a pink, jagged scar that stood out prominently on her dark brown skin. It ran from her left ear to somewhere beneath her collar. Definitely not someone I wanted to tousle with. She could probably snap me in half and use me as a toothpick.

I shrugged, pretending the ceiling was beyond fascinating. "I don't recall." Nor did I want to. I doubted she was a wife of a cheating husband. I'd have remembered her.

She slapped her thigh, and I was certain the echo could be heard all the way in Orange County. "This is going to drive me crazy."

I sighed. God forbid. "Maybe from TV. My face has been plastered all over it for the past few days."

"I seen that. The judge murderer. Good for you. They think they're superior and can boss people around. He probably got what was coming to him."

I swallowed hard, never having met someone so pro-murder before.

"But nah, that ain't it," she argued shaking her head. "I know you from someplace else."

Desperately wanting this game of twenty questions to end, I said, "I'm a PI."

Another slap, or this time it might have been a punch. "That's it!" She shouted so loud, I flinched. "You helped my friend, Tanya, discover her husband's a cheating pig. She got full custody of the kids and made out with a hefty settlement."

I looked over. "Tanya Bridge?"

The linebacker's face broke out into a huge grin. "That's right. You done right by her. She's heard he's remarried and cheating on that wife, too. Some people never change."

She swung her legs onto her bed, leaned back against the wall and closed her eyes. "As far as I'm concerned, you deserve a medal for killing that judge. I'm sure you had a good reason."

If I ended up in prison, I wanted her as a cellmate.

I turned back to the ceiling as she lapsed into silence again.

The worst part about jail - even worse than the canned beans and polyester attire - was that it gave you way too much time to think. Danny, Aiden, and Derek circled through my mind. The men in my life. Depressing thought.

Danny was a question mark. He'd betrayed me, he'd turned me into the cops, he may have even set me up for murder, or at least played a significant part in it. He'd also been my closest friend for more years than I could count. So, who was he really?

Aiden, on the other hand, was much more straightforward. He was The Law. Evidence, proof, do the right thing even if you know that on some level it's the wrong thing. I had to admire that to some extent. My whole life Derek had taught me to work the system, skirt the grey areas of the law in search of the truth. Meeting someone who so honorably stuck to his code of ethics was oddly refreshing. Even if his code currently had me sitting in a cell with Lady Linebacker.

Which brought me to Derek. I wondered what he was doing, what he thought of his daughter now. Ever since I'd taken over the business, I'd felt like he was waiting for me to prove him right, that he hadn't made a mistake entrusting a former model with a P.I. firm. And this wasn't exactly the way to do it.

Then Judge Waterston's face floated to the surface of my conscience. He'd been my big fish, my ticket to staying in the black. But he wasn't actually any different than Tanya's husband. In fact, he'd been even easier to reel in, ready to jump on any chance at infidelity that sashayed his way. While the woman who had hired me was fake, the reason for the hire was real. He had been a cheater as sure as Tanya's husband had.

I was replaying my case file on the judge for the tenth time in my head when a uniformed cop stopped at our cell.

"You still want that phone call, Bond?" His squeaky voice matched his pimply face.

I jumped up. I hadn't been able to get in touch with anyone yesterday and had ended up leaving a message on Caleigh's cell. I nodded vigorously.

He led me to a phone at an empty desk in the squad room and cuffed me to a drawer.

I rolled my eyes. How very dramatic. Did he really think I'd try to escape in a room full of cops?

Well, okay, so maybe I'd *try*.

I cradled the receiver between my ear and shoulder and punched in the numbers to the office. Someone please answer.

On the second ring, Maya's beautiful voice filled my ear. "Bond Agency. Loved one missing? Spouse cheating? We're your shaken and not stirred solution."

We seriously needed to work on that greeting.

"It's Jamie."

"Ohmigod, boss. Are you okay? I'm putting you on speaker." I heard her calling to Sam and Caleigh, heels scurrying closer to the phone.

"I'm fine," I reassured her.

"I'm so sorry I didn't answer," Caleigh voice came on. "After I listened to your message, I called the station, but they wouldn't let me talk to you."

Afraid time would run out and Pimply would wrench the receiver from my hand, I cut her off. "My preliminary hearing is in the morning."

"We'll be there." Sam's words were calm and reassuring. "What do you need?"

"To get out. Bail was denied."

A low gasp circled their end of the call. I prayed they got my message. I assumed conversations on the police phones were recorded, and I couldn't take the chance of elaborating.

It could be months before the trial was scheduled, and there was no way I was staying here that long. Not while the real killer was out there enjoying my share of the fresh air and sunshine.

"What else?" Maya asked.

I paused a moment. Then on a whim answered, "Dig up everything you can on Waterston."

"We already did a profile when we were hired," Maya protested.

"I know. But I need more. Specifically about women he may have worked with, socialized with, belonged to his country club."

"His affairs," Sam concluded.

"Right." While I'd been distracted by the frame-up job (and rightfully so), what this case was really about was one dead judge. And somewhere in his past had to be the arrow pointing to a golden motive.

"Is there anything else we can bring you? Anything you need?" Caleigh asked again.

I shook my head. "No. I'm fine." Which was far from the truth, but I wasn't going down without a fight. "Just get everything you can and be here tomorrow for the hearing."

"You got it, boss," she agreed, then hung up.

I held the silent receiver to my ear a moment longer, crossing my fingers they found something. Something had to give in this case.

And it wasn't going to be me.

* * *

Later that afternoon, after wearing a hole in the tile and listening to Lady Linebacker's numerous stories about life in the 'hood, Pimply Cop returned. I had a visitor.

He led me to a room much like the one I'd seen Aiden in and cuffed my ankles to the metal table. Pumped with excitement that the girls had found something so soon, I practically bounced in the metal chair.

But when the door opened, the grin died on my face. Instead of seeing long legs, flawless skin and hair any woman would kill for, ripped jeans, a five o'clock shadow and a glum expression greeted me.

Derek.

He was the last person I expected to see. He took the chair across from me and immediately reached out and grabbed my hands. He gave a small squeeze and sniffled.

I concentrated hard on not losing it in front of him. Girly girls cried when their dads visited them in prison. P.I.'s didn't.

"What are you doing here?" I asked, glad my voice didn't betray the tears backing up in my throat.

"The one with the legs called and told me."

I laughed, emotion bubbling up from me before I could stop it. "They all have legs, Derek."

A corner of his mouth lifted, and he released my hands, sitting up straight. "Are you alright? You know to cover your face and bob and weave, right?"

I nodded. "I'm fine. This isn't Alcatraz."

"Hey, I've seen prison movies."

"Yeah, rented from a back room for some girl on girl action, right?"

His laughter filled the room, and whether I wanted to admit it or not, it comforted me.

"I called Levine," he told me. "You need a better attorney. You need better than some overworked public defender."

I shook my head. "Levine doesn't do criminal defense."

"Yeah, that's' what he told me, too," Derek said, as if he didn't believe him. All lawyers were the same to Derek - a necessary evil.

"It's okay. The PD is fine."

We both knew that was a load of crap, but what else could I say? Besides, the truth was out there, and my girls were going to uncover it.

He got that distant look in his eyes, as if his thoughts were miles away. "You're just like her, you know."

Was I supposed to know which of his many women he was referring to?

"Who?"

He cupped my hand again. "Your mother."

I held my breath, not expecting that one.

"She wouldn't have wanted me to see her cry either."

Oh hell. That did it. Tears leaked from my eyes.

Derek reached cross the table and brushed one off my cheek. "Buck up, kid," he said, his voice thick. "You're a fighter, just like she was. And we Bonds always come out on top."

God, I prayed he was right.

CHAPTER NINETEEN

———

A bailiff, with skin the color of dark chocolate and a body that cried steroids, ushered me into the gleaming courtroom. Windows ran from mid wall to ceiling, curving at the top. Pieces of stained glass were set in, reminding me of churches. Sun spilled through, warm and comforting, casting shapes of pink, blue, yellow and green on the hardwood floor. A contrast to the scents of Pine Sol and fear that mingled in between the seats and witness stand.

At Santa's request, I'd been allowed to change into my street clothes, but they weren't a whole lot better than the orange jumpsuit. I was dressed for a club, not a hearing, and I could feel all the eyes in the courtroom on me.

Including Aiden's.

He was clean shaven, had on a fresh suit and tie, and if I got close enough probably smelled like clean laundry and subtle aftershave. I, on the other hand, smelled like a woman who hadn't showered in two days. I tried not to let that sway my confidence.

His eyes followed me through the room, the expression hooded and unreadable. Whether he was imagining a swift victory or what kind of undergarments were making the panty-lines on my dress, I had no idea.

The bailiff tugged my arm, pulling me forward to the defendant's table, then removed my cuffs. I took a quick look around the courtroom.

Caleigh and Sam sat in the gallery, behind Aiden, on the prosecution's side. Santa had informed me that it was likely they would eventually be called as state witnesses due to the benefit dinner. Maya, however, was seated right behind me. She wore a long, wavy brown wig and trench coat. Way too hot for July.

If I could sing, I'd belt out Hallelujah.

Near the back of the courtroom sat Candy and Apple, dressed in halter tops and mini skirts, along with several other dancers from The Spotted Pony. A second bailiff stood by the courtroom doors, and Derek sat in the last aisle seat.

I let out a shaky breath as I faced the front of the courtroom, pretending I wasn't aware of him or the girls.

The one person I didn't see here was Danny. I tried not to dwell on what that meant as my PD arrived, dropping a worn leather briefcase on the table in front of him.

He nodded at me, offering a reassuring smile. He looked so jolly all the time I couldn't tell if he genuinely believed in my innocence or was just passing the time until we broke for lunch.

Not that it really mattered.

I felt movement behind me and heard Maya's voice whisper. "We found Alexa White."

The name meant nothing to me. I shook my head slowly.

"She was a member of the Waterston's country club. And she was sleeping with the judge."

Ah. Bingo.

Santa glanced at me then Maya. His bushy white brows formed a straight line.

She cleared her throat, and I felt her lean away from me. The trench rubbed against the wooden seat, making a scratchy noise.

When Santa turned back to his briefcase full of papers again, Maya's breath tickled my shoulder. "Two days before he died they fought. He accusing her of secretly taping their lovemaking. Said he received a video in the mail of the two of them. Anonymous sender."

My body tingled with where this was heading, my mind pulling pieces together as a voice boomed from the front of the room.

"All rise. The Superior Court of Los Angeles County, State of California is now in session."

Chairs scraped across the hardwood floor, and we all stood.

When the judge's chamber door opened and the mean, old kook from the bail hearing stepped forward, I held my breath. Despite the oath of justice and defendants being innocent until proven guilty, I was certain this judge wanted to see me hung from the nearest rafter.

"The Honorable Judge Preston E. Wyatt presiding."

He settled into his chair and glanced at the two tables, then to the file he carried in his stubby fingers.

"Be seated."

As the chairs marred the floor again, Maya tugged my shoulder, bending me back ever so slightly.

"Alexa had no idea what Waterston was talking about, told him so, and he left in a huff. She never saw him again." Maya's words tumbled out in one breath.

The judge looked to me. His dark, angry eyes threatened to nail me to the spot.

Maya feigned a sneeze, sitting quickly.

I sat as well, back upright, shoulders squared, hands folded neatly on the table like a good little girl.

The judge returned his attention to the file.

I wiped the back of my hand across my damp hairline and noticed it shook. I wasn't familiar with this kind of fear. But like everything that had been difficult in life, I pushed it away and focused. There was no room for meltdowns now.

The judge spouted legalese about the fairness of the trial, Santa responded in kind, as did Aiden. He glanced my way as he spoke. The left corner of his mouth tugged up as if to say, hang in there.

I quickly looked away.

"The prosecution calls Daniel Flynn to the stand," Aiden said.

My breath hitched and everything froze for a moment.

Danny was here. Waiting in the wings to put the final nail in my coffin.

I watched the bailiff open the courtroom door. I clenched my hands together, knuckles going white as the bailiff stepped into the hall to call Danny.

Only as the courtroom waited, a wretched moan of pain cut through the silence.

All eyes turned toward Caleigh, as she clutched her chest and fell to the floor.

Suddenly chairs scraped, people gasped, and everyone swarmed toward Caleigh.

Aiden, the front bailiff, Santa, and Maya ran toward her prone form first. Maya wore a yellow sundress and no wig. I glanced to the bench and saw the trench coat and wig on the seat.

Candy, Apple and the other Spotted Pony girls chose that moment to squeal and run over to the other bailiff, jumping, bouncing, squealing, and generally making spectacles of themselves that were hard for any man to ignore.

I took a deep breath.

Then reached over, grabbed Maya's getup, and quickly walked toward the center aisle.

I was near hyperventilation. My internal organs felt unattached, as if they sloshed around in my body cavity.

A beefy hand grabbed my arm, and I tensed.

"Hurry," Derek whispered, then used his body as a shield so I could slip on the disguise.

This wasn't going to work. I'd get caught and be sentenced to the lethal injection without a trial.

I repeated that negative mantra with each shaky step to the door. The three foot distance stretched for miles. When I finally reached it, I took a chance and glanced back.

Caleigh still moaned on the floor.

The dancers ran around like a circus side show.

The judge banged his gavel, shouting, "Order in the court."

Aiden looked up, and our eyes locked.

I told my feet to run, but they didn't listen. His gaze pinned me to the spot, realization dawning in his eyes.

I wasn't the only one who had been set-up.

But he didn't point a finger and yell, "Fugitive." He didn't instruct the bailiffs to chase me down. He didn't say a word. Instead, he just stared.

And I ran.

Out the doors, through the stream of chaos filtering into the courtroom. I almost ran into a pair of medics racing for the courtroom as I headed to the stairs. Hand gripped on the cold, metal railing, I held on for dear life while running, practically falling, down three stories. I tripped on the last step and fell forward. Landing against the door with a smack, I took several deep breaths. Shoulders back, head held high, I swung the door open and stepped into the lobby, trying to look the part of a calm, free citizen, when, in fact, every muscle ached with tension. The sun blinded me for a moment, and when I moved out of the direct glare, my step faltered. Two guards stood beside the metal detectors.

I forced a smile and decided a new mantra was in order.

"I am free. I am free. I am free." The words slipped from my lips like a lover's caress.

To my amazement, they didn't give me a second glance. God bless underpaid government employees.

I pushed through the glass front doors, and sunlight heated my head, making me instantly sweat under the wig. I ran down the concrete steps, onto the sidewalk, and briskly walked to the corner.

Keeping my head down as I walked, I shoved my hands in the trench pockets. They immediately came up against something cool and metal. A set of keys with a rhinestone encrusted M dangling between them. Maya's car keys.

I turned them over in my hand and realized a post-it was stuck to the back of the M. In blue, neat, curved letters, Maya had written: grande, nonfat Caramel Macchiato.

I'll admit, I could go for one right about now.

A siren screeched through the air, and I shoved the keys back in my pocket, my steps quickening. I reached the corner and looked up and down the block. I needed somewhere to hide.

Without thinking, I turned left and crossed the intersection. A car pulled to the side of the road, to allow the sirens through. I hit the opposite curb as the vehicle came into view. It wasn't a patrol car but an ambulance.

Caleigh. It was here because of her fake attack.

I laughed out loud and sprinted down the street. The ambulance passed and stopped in front of the courthouse.

I kept my head down and kept walking.

A burly guy headed toward me, talking into his cell. As we passed one another, I got a whiff of French Roast. I knew my coffee scents.

Wait, coffee. I stopped and glanced back. He held a beige cup with a green logo.

Starbucks.

I looked ahead, and at the next corner stood the most delicious coffeehouse in the entire galaxy.

Five minutes later, I'd found Maya's car in the lot and settled inside. I untied the trench but kept on the wig, just in case. With the car in drive, I pulled onto the street and headed in the opposite direction, toward the freeway.

I drove blindly, forcing my heart rate to settle down as I went over the name Maya had given me in court.

Alexa White.

Two weeks before the judge died, they'd fought. That was telling. Maya said she swore she didn't know what the judge was talking about when he mentioned a sex video, but women didn't always tell the truth. Especially if they were murderers. Maybe she had made the video and had planned to blackmail the judge with it. Maybe something went wrong - he wouldn't pay, threatened to prosecute her for blackmail - and she decided to get rid of him instead.

Of course, the whole theory hinged on whether or not there really was a video. The judge said yes; Alexa said no.

I merged onto the 101, heading north. I wasn't sure where I was going. The cops would be all over my familiar haunts, and it was only a matter of time before they questioned the girls and put an APB out on Maya's car. I had to get off the roads soon.

Assuming the video existed, Waterston must have had a copy of it. He'd seen it, fought with Alexa over it. Had the police gotten hold of it? Possibly, but it didn't sound like they'd been looking for it. And if Waterston had been clever, which all cheating spouses tried to be, then he wouldn't have left it lying around. He would have hidden it. Somewhere safe. Where his real wife wouldn't find it.

Lucky for me, finding things that men kept hidden from their wives was my specialty.

CHAPTER TWENTY

The giant white pillars of the Waterston estate came into view, and I checked all emotion. This was do or die time. The video *had* to be within the walls of the Margaret Mitchell-esque home. I didn't even want to think about the alternative.

I parked far down the road, shrugged off the coat and popped Maya's trunk, hoping to find anything less conspicuous than clubbing attire I was currently rocking.

A tire iron, spare, and small duffel were the only items. I zipped open the bag and discovered a bikini, pair of white socks, a tube of gel toothpaste, a comb, and a yellow blazer. Geeze, what did Maya do in her free time?

I grabbed the blazer and tried to smooth out the wrinkles. I tossed the trench in the trunk, locked everything up and slipped into the jacket. Made from a thin linen, at least I wouldn't melt before I got to the property.

I walked as nonchalantly as I could down the tree-lined street, forcing my nerves away. I held onto Derek's jailhouse assurances that we Bonds were tough. Unbreakable. I *would* find the judge's real killer, and I would *not* be going back to jail. I held onto that thought with a two-fisted death grip as I forced one foot in front of the other.

As I approached the house, a white Mustang pulled up to the gates and drove into the estate.

Great. Company.

I assumed this meant Mrs. Waterston was home. Chances were, with a house that size, domestic staff would be around, too. A house full of people was going to make things a bit more difficult.

Another car pulled onto the property. And then another. I caught a glimpse of the drivers. All women, most young. No passengers. I wondered what Mrs. Waterston was up to.

It was a tad too soon for a garden party, no?

When I reached the gate, a petite brunette walked up from the opposite end of the road. Dressed in a beige pencil skirt with matching jacket and a white blouse, she gave a friendly smile and fell into step with me.

"Are you here for the interview?" she asked. Her voice was high and nervous, resembling Minnie Mouse.

Interview? Interesting.

We passed the open gate and stayed along the shoulder of the driveway, allowing plenty of room for the cars.

"Yes. Are you nervous?" I asked, trying to strike up a camaraderie that might result in loose lips.

Her eyes widened, and she let out a huff, as if feeling relief at telling her biggest secret. "Oh my God, you too?"

In all honesty, I was now more anxious about finding access to the judge's private quarters than anything else. A group of high-strung women vying for the same job was a runway walk. I'd done it all my life. These women, however, could be the perfect ruse or my biggest demise. I'd lay fifty-fifty odds on my luck this afternoon.

She stared at my hands. "Did you forget your resume?"

Right, a resume. I didn't even carry a purse. "I emailed it in," I lied.

She nodded. "Smart. I kept tweaking mine all night. I've actually never worked as a personal assistant before."

Ah. So that was the job.

"But, I do have a lot of experience with the elderly," she went on. "I mean, not that Mrs. Waterston is all that old, but I understand how one needs help with things when one loses a spouse. It must be totally tragic, you know?"

"Totally," I agreed.

"Plus, I really need this job. My landlord won't give me an extension on the rent and..." She trailed off, apparently realizing she was spilling her life story to the competition.

A high-pitched giggle came from Minnie's lips. "Sorry. I tend to ramble when I'm nervous," she said as we reached the front of the house.

"It's okay," I reassured her. "My landlord's an asshole, too."

The front door was open, apparently expecting us, and we stepped into the marble foyer. To our right stood double doors that were shut, and to our left was a large sitting room where other girls gathered. A grand curved staircase set off by a crystal chandelier sat in the center.

I followed Minnie into the sitting room, which was decorated in light, muted tones. Cream sofas, pale blue rugs, several vases of flowers scattered through the room. I took up a spot in the corner, hoping to blend in with a potted plant. If I'd wanted this job, I would've sat dead center, like the blonde seated on the ottoman, giving her best impression of a statue. Today, however, I couldn't risk Mrs. Waterston stepping in and recognizing me.

Rubber-soled shoes squeaked on the polished floor. A stocky woman in an actual black and white maid's uniform appeared at the door. "Mrs. Waterston will see you now," she said, addressing the blonde.

The girl took a deep breath, then followed her.

When they walked out, I stepped forward to see where they went. The maid opened the double doors across the foyer and ushered the girl inside. With just a quick glance, it appeared to be a study, the corner of a dark, mahogany desk and shelves filled with leather bound books visible before the door shut.

It didn't strike me as having the same feminine decorating hand as the room I was currently in. If I had to guess, it was the domain of the late judge.

Which meant that was were I needed to go.

Okay, Jamie, think. Clearly I needed the place to myself. And clearly that wasn't going to happen until Mrs. Waterston was done interviewing her dozen hopeful assistants-to-be. I didn't think yelling "fire" was going to clear the place effectively. And if I couldn't get everyone out, I'd have to wait for them to leave on their own.

I turned to Minnie. "Do you know where the restroom is?"

She shook her head.

Of course not.

"It's just down the hall," said a red-head in a pantsuit. "The second door. You don't want the first. I almost tumbled down the basement stairs. They really should label those doors."

"Thanks." I winked at Minnie, said a silent prayer for her to get the job, and walked into the hall.

I stepped lightly, making sure my heels didn't click too loudly. Wherever the maid had disappeared to, I didn't want to draw her attention.

The restroom door was ajar. I made out the edge of a sink and a glare from a mirror. But I had no intention of hiding out in a half-bath. Chances of getting caught were excellent.

Instead, I grabbed the knob of the first door and twisted. The idea of spending several hours in a dark basement wasn't on the top of my list, but sometimes this job called for filth and grit.

* * *

Thankfully I'd skipped the jail's not-so-scrumptious breakfast of bread, oatmeal, and what passed for coffee that morning. If not, I'd probably have been doing the potty dance hours ago. Then again, if I hadn't my stomach wouldn't have been growling so loudly. I'd swear the last remaining interviewees above must have thought there was a monster underground.

A floorboard squeaked. It was definitely above me, but just in case, I took my feet off the cement floor and sat one step higher. I had no idea how long I'd been waiting. I think I dozed off a couple of times. The sounds upstairs had diminished, but I didn't want to investigate until I heard no movements, even if it meant sneaking around after Mrs. Waterston went to bed.

Being raised in California, basements weren't my thing. They were rare here, usually small, always dusty, dark, and holding untold creepy-crawlies in their corners.

Despite the heat outside and the warm moisture down here, I hugged myself against an internal chill. I couldn't make out much in the darkness, but my sight adjusted enough to see shapes. It appeared empty. Cold. Dank.

Footsteps grew closer. These weren't the maid's soft soles. They were harder, like heels, and slower than any of the girls I'd heard traipsing across the hall earlier.

"Take the rest of the day off, Clarice," I heard above me. I instantly recognized Veronica's smoke-seduced voice.

"Are you sure? I'm happy to stay later if there's anything you wish, Madame." The softer voice was definitely the maid.

They must have been just above me, because the voices were clear as day.

"That's not necessary. I'm having dinner at my sister's. When I return, I'll be heading straight to bed. Unfortunately, my headache has not faded."

"Very well then. Good night."

I listened to two pairs of footsteps move in opposite directions. This was it. Finally my chance. I stood up and shook out the pins and needles in my limbs. My butt was numb too, but that would have to wear off on its own.

I waited until I heard the front door shut twice, then climbed the stairs and eased open the door. The hall was darker than before, but a steady glow of orange sunset filtered in from the glass panels that flanked the front door.

I hurried down the hall to the study, hoping Veronica had left her husband's things exactly as they were. In a twenty-plus year marriage, I prayed she wouldn't want to donate to charity for some time.

Just as I expected, the room was filled with mahogany furnishings that looked slick with a high shine. Someone needed to give Clarice a raise. She'd win the Gold in polishing.

It smelled of expensive perfume, cigarette smoke, and old money.

A quick glance out the window showed no cars parked out front or near the three-car garage, bathed now in hues of orange, gold and pink. Apparently, I'd been in the basement for most of the day. I suddenly wondered how Caleigh and the others were. Had they been carted to the precinct for questioning? Was Aiden out hunting me down with his bloodhounds? If not now, I knew it was only a matter of time.

I blocked out that cheery thought and focused on the task at hand. I started with the desk, searching through drawers. Each one opened easily, no locks, no secret folders taped beneath or stuffed behind. Paper, envelopes, pens, old Christmas cards, a book of holiday stamps—everything neat and organized. No bills, credit card statements, or other personal items.

The computer's desktop held household folders: gardener, housekeeping, catering, etc. Each one was password protected. A recent browser history brought up several employment agencies, divulging where the girls came from. And everything prior to Sunday pertained to various charities, some home decorating sites, and gardening sites. Damn. This felt more like a shared study than Mr. Waterston's private lair.

So where did the late judge keep his secrets?

I pushed back the oversized, leather chair and eyed a file cabinet in the corner.

I tried the drawers, but each was locked. No surprise.

Frustrated, but not defeated, I headed to the back of the house. I passed a large dining room, another sitting room, and finally entered a gleaming, white kitchen. I quickly glanced around, looking for any object sharp enough to pop a lock. A butcher block on a far counter held my answer, and I grabbed a paring knife. I eyed a tempting banana in the fruit basket, but chose to let my hunger wait and headed back into the hall. When this was over I was treating myself to a celebratory dinner of lobster and all the martinis I could handle. To hell with the Bond Agency's finances.

But as I stepped over the threshold from the kitchen, my eye caught a glint of light behind a second staircase. I paused, moving behind the massive structure, and noticed a door. Sunlight streamed from beneath it, forming an orange welcome mat against the floor.

I slowly turned the knob, and peeked in.

What must've once been the help's quarters decades ago was now a fully outfitted man cave. On the far side, a couple of brown leather recliners faced a large flat screen television, surround sound system, and gaming equipment. I smiled at the image of the old man rocking back and forth in one of those chairs while playing Halo.

A desk with laptop and chair stood directly across from the door. A picturesque window flanked the left wall, displaying a fantastic view of the flower garden and a glistening, in-ground pool.

Now this looked like the judge's lair.

I slipped the paring knife into a jacket pocket and opened the bottom cabinet of the entertainment shelving, searching through twenty or so home movies. Each was labeled with name, date, and major players of event. Unfortunately, none were marked: Alexa and Perv Sex Video.

The DVD player turned up empty, so I combed through the desk. Not only was Waterston an X-box fan, but it seemed he loved to doodle. Pages and pages of female bodies sporting various exaggerated body parts filled the desk. If some weren't so vulgar, they'd actually be artistic.

I turned on the computer and loaded the few CDs displayed on his shelves. None of them led to homemade movies.

The sun had set. The sky, a pale grey, would soon turn dark. I had no idea how long Veronica's dinner would be, but I was burning time fast.

I placed the last CD into its case and slipped it back into its plastic holder on the shelf. Only, unlike the others, it didn't fit snugly but stuck out. I pushed again, but it didn't budge. Pulling the CD out, I stared into its slot. It was too dark to see what was in the way.

With a pen, I jabbed the area and hit something. I turned the holder around, pried off the backing, and heard a clank. I pulled the pieces apart and stared at the desk.

A flash drive.

Jackpot!

I thumbed off the plastic top and pushed it into the laptop's USB port. There was only one file, titled: at0429. I double clicked it and everything froze for a moment.

I wasn't sure what I expected. It seemed that every time I thought I was getting closer to the truth, I ended up slammed into a dead end face first. I was tired of getting my hopes up without concrete results. But my hands still shook with anticipation as I watched the QuickTime logo flash across the screen.

A moment later, heavy breathing filled the room. The camera angle was high, like on a closet shelf or the top of an armoire, but with the dozen candles set on the nightstands and dresser, it was easy to make out the couple's profiles.

And their positions.

A curvalicious blonde straddled an older guy. His face was hidden between her perky bosoms. He squeezed her butt then lifted his beet red face and lay back against the pillows.

Yep, definitely Judge Waterston.

She grabbed the top of the brass headboard and bounced. Without jiggle.

They dirty-talked for a few minutes then flipped positions. With her stilettos pointed to the ceiling, she squealed, and I did my best to hold down yesterday's jailhouse delicacies.

Assuming this was Alexa, this had to be the sex video that sent Judge Waterston into a rage. I watched, trying my best at detachment as the two seemed completely absorbed in each other. So absorbed, I realized, that their faces barely made it on screen. There had just been that one fleeting glimpse of the judge. Which was odd. I mean, if Alexa had set up the filming, wouldn't she be trying to position him so that his blackmail-worthy face was front and center? But she seemed almost unaware of where the camera was. I hated to admit it, but maybe Alexa had told my girls the truth. Maybe she really didn't know anything about the video.

So who did?

I tried to make out the decor around the two gyrating bodies. There was the brass bed, a plain wall behind, hard to tell the color in the dim lighting. The pillowcases were striped, and a floral comforter bunched itself at the end of the bed.

I sucked in a breath.

The floral. The brass. I knew this room.

This was Dakota's guest room.

A million questions swirled through my head all at once, jumbled thoughts vying for space as pieces slowly dropped into place.

The answer was on the tip of my brain, when a faint reflection in the monitor caught my attention.

I spun around.

A moment too late.

Light exploded behind my eyes as a resounding whack filled my skull.

CHAPTER TWENTY-ONE

———

I grabbed my head and groaned. The ringing and pounding sounded like a marching band, out of sync. Every inch of my body shivered, including my bones. I was on a hard, cold surface. The ground? It smelled and felt damp, musty, and old. Was I back in Veronica's basement?

Images came flooding back to me: sitting in the man cave, finding the sex video, getting whacked on the head. I rolled onto my side, and another groan leaked from my mouth.

I opened one eye first then the other. It was dark but not as black as when I was down here earlier. A source of light emitted from behind me—a casement window.

The moon.

It illuminated the center of the room. The corners remained dark, but I still made out a large object draped with a sheet, an old sewing machine, and some boxes. Definitely a basement, but not where I waited earlier today. If this even was the same day. There were no stairs, but I noticed a door with a shiny, gold knob.

It called to me like a beacon.

Palms on ground, I pushed up into a sitting position. The room swam, gentle ripples of concrete and moonlight. I wanted to lie back down, close my eyes, and fall into a blissful sleep.

Instead, I rose onto my knees and moaned. My knee still felt sore. In fact, all of my bones felt achy, as if I'd rolled down a flight of stairs.

On unsteady feet, the room swayed again, like a leaning ship. I put out my hands and wobbled into the wall beneath the window. Back and palms pressed against it, I shut my eyes and gulped deep breaths of air.

Nausea rose from the pit of my stomach into my chest. I didn't know a lot about concussions, but I vaguely recalled these were the signs. I took a couple of deep breaths; then I ventured off the wall and headed to the door.

Put one foot in front of the other, Jamie. You can do this. It's like riding a bike.

Except that I sucked at bike riding. Oh, I knew how, and coordination was never an issue. For some reason though, I never enjoyed it. All gangly legs and arms, it always felt unnatural, like crawling after you learned to walk.

I reached the door, grabbed the knob, its metal cold, and twisted.

Nothing.

It was locked. Damn.

My first instinct was to bang my fists on the door and cry for help. But I had no idea who had hit me, or if he was still nearby. As much as I'd love a swift rescue, I needed the element of surprise.

I pressed my ear to the door, listened for footsteps or any sounds. There weren't any. Just complete silence. Then I turned and headed back to the window.

There weren't any sounds from outside either.

No traffic, no animals, nothing.

On tippy-toe, I peeked out the window. All I could make out was grass and the bottom of a bush.

So where the hell was I? And more importantly, who had put me here?

I strained through my aching brain. It would have had to have been someone with access to the Waterston estate. The maid? Why would she knock me out, though? Call the cops and have me arrested? Yes. But resort to violence and then lock me up? Doubtful.

Was this the work of Dakota and her partner?

Sweat broke out along my back, despite the chill. No. Danny may have set me up, but he wouldn't hurt me. I knew this. Dakota... her I wasn't so sure about.

I pushed on the glass window, trying to pop it out, but it didn't budge. I briefly contemplated trying to break it and climb out, but it looked loud, and I didn't know how far away my captor was. If he heard it shatter, there was no telling how quickly he'd come running.

If it was a he.

Instead, I surveyed my surroundings for anything I could use as a weapon when he came back. I walked to the item with the sheet and ripped off the cloth. It was a full-length mirror on a wooden, swivel stand. I tried not to gasp at my sight, hair matted at the sides and sticking up on top, complexion the color of ash, sunken eyes with dark rings, as if I'd been in a boxing ring. Not pretty. I moved on.

The sewing machine was too heavy to be of much use, especially in my condition. The boxes were partially empty with only old fabric and spools of thread inside. Nothing sharp, dangerous, or menacing.

Okay, if I couldn't fight him, I had to outsmart him. I looked from the window to the pile of junk again. I could break the glass in the window, then hide. Behind the mirror. Then when my captor ran out to look for me, I'd sneak out the door.

It was flimsy as plans went, but it was the best I had.

I pulled off one of my stilettos and wobbled to the window. With my left hand covering my eyes, I used all my might and swung. The pointy heel made contact with the glass but only left a nick.

Great, I'd be doing this all night. The aim was difficult too. I had to balance on my toes. Too bad I hadn't taken ballet lessons. And with one shoe off and the state of my head, it made balancing almost impossible.

I struck out again and again. Sometimes I'd hit the sill, or scrape my knuckles on the cement. Finally, the heel cracked the glass. Hope jumped into my throat. One more whack, and I'd have it. I cocked my arm back.

And the door swung open, hitting the back wall with a thud.

I jumped and twisted, nearly stumbling forward.

The doorway stood dark, but a figure took a step toward the moonlight. The scent of perfume and cigarette smoke trickled in.

Another step, and I spotted brown slippers, thick calves and the hem of a skirt.

"What do you want?" I asked, squinting to make out a face in the darkness.

She took another step, and my breath hitched, making my chest burn.

"You annoying twit," she said.

Bathed in a whitish glow, Veronica Waterston pointed a gun at me.

CHAPTER TWENTY-TWO

———

I gripped my shoe so tightly the buckle dug into my palm. I ignored the pain and focused on the lunatic in front of me.

The wife.

As I stared at the barrel of her gun catching the moonlight, pieces fell into places with sudden clarity. I'd spent so much time looking at the *fake* Mrs. Waterston, that I'd never considered the *real* one.

"You couldn't just be as dumb as you look, could you?" Veronica's tone was raspy, deep, with an undertone of anger bubbling just beneath the surface.

I paused. The key ingredient to staying alive in a hostage situation, at least according to television, was to keep the person with the gun talking instead of shooting.

"I look dumb?" I asked, clearly not caring what she thought, but hoping to stall her.

She grinned, showing off a row of stained teeth. "A model who wears inappropriate shoes to work, and is a bleached blonde."

Hey! I took offense to that. My hair color was all my own, thank you very much.

"So, that's why you chose me. You thought the dumb blonde would be easy to frame?"

She waved me off. "Don't flatter yourself. You were a random name in the P.I. section of Yelp. A means to an end."

"The end being killing your husband," I said slowly, watching her reaction.

But if she felt anything, she hid it well. Her face remained relaxed and impassive, as if she were discussing a ladies' luncheon instead of her husband's murder. "I'd had enough. I was finished with him."

"Enough what?" I asked, trying to keep her talking, as I scanned the area behind her. She'd left the door open. A means of escape. If I could catch her off guard, there was a chance I could slip past her to freedom.

Her eyes narrowed. "You know very well, enough what."

"Women?" I asked, hazarding a very educated guess.

She grinned again, a flat thing that held no actual humor. "Well, he certainly wasn't giving a lesson on court proceedings to the bimbo on the video, now was he?"

No, he wasn't. And the fact that she knew that, meant she had seen the video.

"Alexa White," I said.

The wife nodded, the gun bobbing up and down in her hand as well. "Just the latest in a long line of bimbos over the years."

"How did you get the video?" I asked, genuinely curious this time.

"It's what I'd call a fortunate accident," she informed me. "His niece, Dakota, was putting a strain on our finances. Always calling, looking for money. I told my husband not to give in to her outrageous demands, but he spoiled her. Even to the point of turning a blind eye to her less than legal activities."

"Such as?"

"I suspected she was using drugs."

Good guess.

"But my husband wouldn't believe it," she continued. "So I had someone set up cameras around her apartment. I figured if I caught her in the act, my husband couldn't ignore her shortcomings any longer, and he'd cut off her money supply."

"But you didn't catch Dakota," I prompted, remembering the floral sheets in the judge's homemade porn.

Her mouth drew into a tight line, her eyes darkening. Here was the emotion I'd been expecting earlier. Betrayal, hurt, and pure anger.

"No. I caught him using Dakota's apartment as his personal love nest. How dare he betray me! How dare he humiliate me like that. It was one thing to suspect what he was really doing all of those late nights he spent on 'committees,'" she said, doing air-quotes with her fingers. Which, incidentally took the gun off of me for a second. I paused, feeling a chance for escape in my future. The more she talked about her late cheating husband, the less she focused on her current captive.

"But it was another thing entirely," she went on, "to watch it myself."

"You must have been so angry," I said.

"Damned right I was angry!" she shouted, bubbles of spittle forming at the corners of her mouth, making her resemble a rabid dog.

"So you had to do something."

"Exactly. I couldn't let him get away with that. Not with rubbing it in my face like that."

"Why not just divorce him?" I asked. "You had solid evidence."

She laughed, her eyes blazing. "I was humiliated enough. I was not going to give him the satisfaction of publicly humiliating me again by raking my name through his sleazy affairs. Playing out a public divorce in the press was out of the question."

"So you decided to kill him."

She didn't answer, her eyes just looking past me, into some moment I couldn't see. Possibly the one where she'd shot the life out of her husband.

I took a small step to the left, my eye on the open door. But the movement snapped Veronica back to reality, the gun going straighter in her hand.

"And that's where I came in," I said, trying to steer back to friendly conversation as I eyed her trigger finger. It was scary tense.

She nodded. "Yes. I needed to make sure I had a perfect scapegoat."

"But why me?"

"You make a living off of adulterers like my husband," she said, very matter-of-factly. "I found that ironically satisfying."

I didn't point out that I made my living *catching* cheating men to benefit women like her.

"So you hired Donna to impersonate you? Why go through the trouble?" But even as I asked the question, I knew the answer. Deniability.

"While she was at your office, I was at a luncheon for the Rose Society committee. In case she botched it, I'd have no idea why that fool was impersonating me."

How clever.

"How did you convince her?" I asked, moving to the left just another inch.

"It wasn't hard," she bragged. "I found the letters she'd written to my husband, urging him to overturn his ruling in her husband's case, at first. Later they blamed him for the man's death. She hated my husband as much as I did, and I'd dare say she loved money almost as much. She was happy to play a role for me without asking too many questions."

"So, you had her hire me, giving yourself an alibi and planting evidence against me."

Those yellow teeth made an appearance again as a smile stretched across her wrinkled cheeks. "You have to admit, it was rather clever of me. I had Donna wear oiled gloves during your first meeting, remember? When you shook her hand, your fingerprints were transferred onto them. Then it was a simple job of applying them to the murder weapon. Coupled with the surveillance video, it was a perfect setup."

I had to agree; it was ideal.

"So why kill Donna?" I asked,

She gave me a hard look. "You think years of being a criminal court justice's wife has taught me nothing? I had to tie up lose ends."

"So you stole your niece's pills?"

"*Stole*? She lied to us to pay for those. She stole that money from me."

An interesting take on it, but I let it go.

"You thought of everything," I said, throwing a compliment her way instead.

She nodded. "Yes. I did." Then a frown creased her forehead. "But you had to get in the way. You couldn't just play along like the little puppet you were. No. First, you find Donna, then you finally get arrested and do what? Escape." She threw the word out with disgust.

"Guess I'm not so blonde now after all, huh?" I couldn't help pointing out.

Which, in hindsight might not have been the smartest move.

Her eyes narrowed. "Oh, we'll see about that," she promised, taking a step closer to me, closing any distance I'd put between us, gun pointed right at her target.

The gun still remained steady. I'd no doubt that if she killed her husband and an innocent actress in cold blood, shooting me would be easy.

My throat felt like I drank a cup of sand. I swallowed hard, but it didn't do much good.

"How will you explain my body?" I asked, almost choking on the word "body" as a self-reference.

She grinned. "Actually, this is the best of all plans, and it fell right into my lap. You lied your way into my home, which several witnesses saw. You were snooping around my late husband's personal belongings, likely looking for the sex video he made with you."

"He never made a-" I started, then realized it didn't matter. Who were the police going to believe? The grieving widow who did, indeed, have a sex video of her husband and another woman, or my prone corpse?

"I walked in and caught you, you attacked me, and I shot you in self-defense."

Damn. She was right. That story was great.

"Now, let's take a walk back to my husband's den where this tragic accident all takes place," she suggested.

As much as I was yearning to walk through that door behind her, I knew if I did it with her, I was a dead woman. I was out of time, out of options, and acting on pure instinct.

"No," I protested.

Veronica paused, her eyebrows drawing together in a frown again. "Excuse me, but you're not in a position to argue."

"You're overlooking something," I told her, feeling adrenalin surge in my belly.

She raised the gun to eye level. "What's that?"

I stepped to the left then the right, in jerking movements. "You're directly in the light."

I lifted my arm and chucked the shoe in my hand, pulling a muscle in my shoulder from the force.

It spun through the air, creating a whoosh sound. The heel whacked her in the forehead then clanked on the floor.

She yelped. One hand flew to her face.

And I took off.

CHAPTER TWENTY-THREE

———

I charged past Veronica and ran through the door. Darkness surrounded me, and I realized I was now in the section of the basement I waited in this afternoon. I'd never seen the door to a separate room.

My ankle hit the stairs, and I fell to my hands and knees. I scrambled to my feet and scampered to the top landing. Veronica's footsteps were heavy behind me. Her breathing was fast and uneven. Bet she regretted those cigarettes now.

I hit the main hallway and spied the front door. I could run for it, but I knew there was precious little to hide behind outside. And with Veronica hot on my tail, I was no match for the speed of her bullets. Even in the dark, I didn't want to take my chances that her aim was that bad.

Instead, I lunged for the alarm system beside the door. I hit the emergency button, praying someone on the other end would summon the police. Then I ran upstairs, taking two steps at a time, in search of a hiding place to wait out their arrival.

Panic soared as I heard Veronica hit the hallway behind me. I climbed higher in a lopsided stride with one shoe off, one on. I ran past bedroom after bedroom, choosing the master at the end of the hallway. It was located in the back right corner of the house, and I sighed in relief as I stepped inside. There were plenty of places to hide. The shower, under the four-poster bed, the walk-in closets.

I noticed the balcony and opened the French doors. There was only two feet of space, and no way down. Below lay the pool. A long ways down.

Leaving the doors ajar, I turned to the bathroom. I searched the cabinets for a weapon but found nothing more toxic than hemorrhoid cream and hot rollers.

I pulled my arms out of Maya's jacket, hot and suffocating in my escape, and tossed it aside. It hit the floor with a tinny, metallic sound.

I grabbed it and rifled through the pockets. The pairing knife I'd picked up earlier. I said a silent thank you to the gods of thorough snooping.

The bedroom door opened. Veronica wheezed in the doorway, a shrill whistling sound. She clearly wasn't used to running after people.

I slipped behind the bathroom door, knife clutched in hand. The closet doors opened, hangers rattled. She went onto the balcony then hesitated outside the bathroom before the door squeaked open another inch.

I flattened myself against the wall, feeling the knife shake in my hand. I glanced through the space between the hinges, terrified I'd see her beady eyes staring back.

I saw Veronica's arm extend, her hand peek around the doorframe, gun pointed ahead of her. One more step and she'd be inside, staring me down.

I reacted on instinct, brought up the knife and slashed the back of her hand.

Blood oozed from the cut. Drops splattered on the floor, and the gun fell. A half-yell-half-groan came from deep within her chest, and she quickly drew her arm back.

I kicked the gun before she could reach down for it, then pushed on the door, hoping to knock her out of the way and give myself a moment to grab the better weapon.

She must've regained her footing fast, though, because she pushed back. For an older woman, she was stronger than I thought.

The door slammed me into the wall. The knife fell from my hand and clanked to the floor.

I wiggled onto my hands and knees, aiming for the gun. But before I could grab it, Veronica rammed into me. I skidded across the travertine tile and slammed into a claw foot tub.

She moved fast, too fast, and slipped, grabbing onto the edge of the sink. That calm, reassured presence she'd had in the basement was gone. Her pupils were dilated, her complexion splotchy. She bent toward the gun.

I sprang up and ran to it.

We both arrived at the same time, but her fingers wrapped around the pearl-covered handle first.

No, I screamed in my head.

I wouldn't say my life passed before my eyes as I watched her raise the gun to meet me. No images of Mom, Derek, my girls or even Danny. Instead, I thought of Donna. Her lifeless expression. The way Veronica had used her then cast her aside when she was no longer needed.

This lunatic didn't care that Donna had a life, was grieving for a man she loved. How could she when she thought so little of her own husband's life? Yes, he cheated. So have plenty of other men. You get divorced, take the bastard for everything he owns. You didn't elaborately plan his murder.

And there was no way I was going to let her get away with that.

Without thinking, I reacted. I grabbed Veronica's wrist with both my hands, pushing the gun away from me. She struggled back, the both of us pulling and pushing, trying to get the other to let go. Our arms ended above our heads, the gun pointed at the ceiling. Unfortunately she was only an inch shorter than me, so neither of us had the upper hand.

But I had one additional weapon she did not.

I lifted my one still-shoed foot and slammed the heel onto her slipper.

She screamed, her fingers slipping.

I yanked the gun free and stepped back. My chest heaved with uneven breaths as I pointed the barrel at her.

But like a frickin' bull, she charged toward me.

I raised the gun, pretended she was a paper target, and pulled the trigger.

The shot rang out. Deafening.

Veronica's eyes widened. She clutched her lower abdomen as bright red blood seeped through her fingers.

My stomach retched, as I blinked in disbelief that almost matched hers. I hadn't aimed to kill. I hadn't aimed at all, just fired out of pure instinct and self preservation.

She staggered, the back of her knees hitting the edge of the tub. Her feet slipped out from beneath her, and she fell backward, landing in the tub.

The irony of how the end of her reign of terror resembled Donna's demise didn't escape me.

I rubbed my face with my free hand, stunned, somehow unable to move. I'm not sure how long I stood like that, in a state of semi-shock. I vaguely registered sirens in the distance, the front door opening, and feet pounding up the stairs.

"Jamie?" I heard as the footsteps approached the doorway.

I turned and found Aiden standing there, two uniformed cops beside him, guns drawn. But Aiden's features were soft, concerned, eyes roving my person for wounds.

"I'm sorry," I squeaked out. "But, this time I really did shoot someone, Aiden."

CHAPTER TWENTY-FOUR

———

Two days later, I stood outside the Bond Agency, staring at the letters embossed on the door. I traced them with my finger, not ready to go inside and face what waited for me.

After an ambulance had taken Veronica away (who, incidentally was not dead, but definitely severely wounded), and the police had questioned me, I was taken to the hospital, where I spent the night due to my concussion. The next day I was released, and after a quick message to all that I was alive and fine, I turned off my phone, took a bubble bath until the bubbles were gone and water was cold, and snuggled in my bed. Where I'd stayed for the next twenty-four hours.

Now, however, it was back to work, back to making this business operate in the black, and back to restoring what little reputation we might have left.

I took a deep breath and pulled open the door.

"Surprise!"

Caleigh, Maya, Sam, Levine, and, most surprisingly of all, Danny raised cups of Starbucks coffee and cheered.

I blinked, taking in the scene. The lobby was decorated in red and white streamers and matching balloons, imprinted with the word "Congratulations". A round bakery cake with white frosting, yellow and green flowers, and a couple of candles sat beside a stack of paper plates on Maya's desk. Hung on the far wall, facing the front door, was a handmade sign. Written with a black Sharpie, it read: Congrats Super Boss.

Four smiling faces stared back at me, expecting a reaction. One face stared back at me with a sheepish, downcast look as if he'd been dragged here against his will. I chose to ignore Danny, and focused on my girls instead.

"Wow, this is... wow," I repeated myself, closing the door behind me.

Maya handed me a grande, nonfat Caramel Macchiato. "Here you go, boss. Your usual. We thought about buying champagne but figured you'd enjoy this more."

She knew me so well.

"To the bravest ex-model-turned-private investigator ever," Sam said.

Caleigh batted her lashes, as she added, "And the sexiest ex-jailbird."

"Who knows how to maim and not kill." Sam winked.

I chuckled. Long. Hard. Man, it felt great.

Caleigh lit the candles on the cake and said, "Make a wish."

"Aren't wishes only for birthdays?"

"Who cares. You earned one. Or a hundred," Caleigh replied.

I walked to the table and closed my eyes. I thought of my amazing girls and this awesome job, and blew out the candles. I enjoyed modeling. Nothing could beat traveling and shooting at exotic locations, and the money wasn't shabby. But there was a different, deeper thrill when I handed over incriminating evidence to a hurt, broken spouse. My contribution to helping the community.

Everyone clapped, and Sam lifted a knife and began slicing the decadent looking confection.

The phone rang, and Maya rushed to it.

Sam slapped a slice of cake on a plate and handed it to me. "Just so you know, the last ten minutes have been the longest the phone hasn't rung all morning," she informed me.

"Word is out that Bond Agency is the best." Caleigh swiped a finger across her frosting then licked it off.

"Wait-" I said, holding up a hand. "What do mean they know it's the best?"

Caleigh blinked at me. "Like, they know you caught Judge Waterston's *real* killer."

"And that no one gets away with any funny business where Jamie Bond is concerned," Sam said, grinning from ear to ear.

"And," Maya, added, hanging up the phone, "every suspicious wife in town now wants you on *her* side."

"And some husbands," Sam added. "Including Mr. Peters, who was so grateful to find out the truth about his wife that his lawyer dropped off a big fat check yesterday afternoon."

I couldn't help it. I grinned too.

"So, I guess we're in the black," I said, shooting Levine a victorious look.

"Let's wait and see what this month's numbers look like," he hedged. Very lawyerly of him. But, I could see a hint of a smile tugging at the corner of his mouth, too. No matter what this month's numbers said, my three girls were staying.

"So, how do things look for the nefarious Mrs. Waterston?" Levine asked, changing the subject.

"She's recovering well," I said, relaying the info the police had given me that morning on the phone as I dug into my cake. "In the prison hospital, of course. The police found the sex video between Alexa and the judge, as well as a baggie of Shooting Stars with the wife's prints all over them. There was a twenty thousand dollar withdrawal from her account a week before Waterston's death. And the same amount showed up in Donna's account the day after he died. It sounds like they have a pretty strong case."

"I can't believe the lengths some people go to," Caleigh said.

"The betrayal, the dishonesty," Sam added.

I stole a glance at Danny. He was studiously avoiding my gaze, hanging near the back of the room.

The phone rang again, and Maya jumped toward it, a radiant smile on her face. "I hope you're prepared for a busy week, boss."

"I can think of nothing I'd love more." And I totally meant that.

The girls took that as their cue to take coffees and cake to their desks and get to work. Levine mumbled a good-bye and a promise to be back in a couple of weeks to take a look at our accounts receivables. And Danny quietly set his cake down and headed for the door.

"Not so fast," I told him under my breath, grabbing him by the arm.

He paused, looking me in the eyes for the first time since I'd walked in the door. His were a deep, forest green today. Clouded and unreadable.

"I want to talk to you," I told him in a tone that broached no argument.

And for once, he didn't give me one, nodding and following me into my office. I shut the door behind him, then leaned my butt against my desk, crossed my arms over my chest, and sipped my coffee.

Danny watched me, his expression guarded. "So what is this about?"

"I want the truth out of you."

He opened his mouth to speak, but I ran over him.

"The *whole* truth this time, Danny. None of that dancing around denial bullshit you did at your apartment."

Despite the awkward tension in the air, the corner of his mouth quirked upward at my candor. "Fair enough. What do you want to know?"

"How do you know Dakota?"

"We worked together on a few shoots."

"And you slept with her?"

He nodded slowly, as if unsure what the right answer to that was. "Once. But that was awhile ago, back when I first met her."

"Define awhile?"

"Do you really want to know details?" he asked.

No, I didn't. In fact, the image of Danny peeling cheap leopard print lingerie off of Dakota was the last thing I wanted burned into my brain. "What I really want to know," I said, shifting gears, "is that you knew she was Judge Waterston's niece all along."

Again with the slow nod. "I did."

"Christ, Danny, why didn't you tell me?" I asked, slamming my coffee down on the desk.

"I didn't want you to get hurt."

I gave him a get real look. "Seriously? So lying to me is your way of showing you care."

"Yes," he said, his eyes dead serious, his jaw tense, a frown of honest concern between his brows.

Which put a damper on my sarcasm. I crossed my arms again and waited for him to go on.

He sighed, running a hand through his hair. "Look, I'm sorry I had to lie to you. But you were being reckless, and there was a killer out there with your name on her list. As soon as Maya found the Shooting Stars connection, I knew Dakota had to be mixed up in this somehow."

"Wish *I'd* known it then. Would have saved me a lot of trouble."

Danny shook his head. "No, you would have gone to your friendly A.D.A. or, worse yet, gone in guns blazing."

I didn't respond. Mostly because he was kinda right.

"Anyway," he went on, "I asked Dakota to meet me so I could find out what was going on. She did, we talked, and that's when you saw her leaving my place."

"What did she say?" I couldn't help my curiosity getting the better of me.

"About what you'd expect. At first she denied knowing anything about Shooting Stars. Which anyone who knows her knows full well is bullshit. So, when I pressed, she confessed that she was addicted. She said she was trying to quit."

"But not that her aunt had taken some of her supply to kill Donna?"

Danny shrugged. "Honestly, I'm not sure she noticed it was gone. The girl isn't the brightest bulb to begin with, and add being high half the time to that? Anything could slip past her."

"Boy, you sure know how to pick 'em."

He smiled. The first genuine one I'd seen in a long time. "Thanks, James."

I sighed, some of the tension having eased out of the room. Some.

"Okay, maybe I can forgive you for that," I said. "But there is the little matter of your tip to the police about my meeting with Aiden in the park."

Danny chewed the inside of his cheek. "He told you about that, huh?"

"Danny! You tried to get me thrown in jail!"

"Which would have been the safest place for you," he countered. "I needed to make sure you were out of harm's way while I talked to Dakota and tried to find out who was framing you."

I narrowed my eyes at him. "They made me wear orange polyester, Danny."

"I'm sorry."

"And eat baked beans."

"Really sorry."

"And room with the female version of a tattooed linebacker."

Danny took a step forward, his eyes going serious again. "I mean it, Jamie. I'm sorry," he said. And I could tell he really did. "You gotta believe I hated keeping stuff from you. But if anything had happened to you-"

"Something did happen to me, Danny," I cut him off. "I was arrested, thrown in jail, escaped, went on the run, and was almost murdered. And look," I said, gesturing to myself. "I'm fine. Unharmed. I'm a big girl, and I can take care of myself."

Danny smiled, let out a chuckle on a huff of air. "I know, I know. You're a tough guy."

"Damned straight."

"It's just-" He took another step forward. "-James, you're more than a friend to me. I think of you as a..."

He paused, searching for the right word.

A week ago, I would have thought he'd end that sentence with "little sister". But as his brain worked over the possibilities, I watched his gaze go dark and warm, forest green melting into a softer, sea green. His lips parted. Emotion backed up behind his eyes. This was not the look of a big brother. Or a best friend. This was something different. Deeper. More dangerous.

I felt a warm sensation curling in my stomach, blood suddenly pumping in my ears as I waited for him to finish the thought.

"Yes?" I asked, realizing I was slightly breathless.

"Well, you're very important to me," he finally said, his voice thick and low.

I swallowed and locked eyes with him. A million things were swimming there, unspoken. Though, whether I was ready for him to speak them or not, I wasn't sure.

Not that I had a say in the matter. Danny quickly broke the gaze, breaking the moment with it, and took a giant step back, clearing his throat.

"So... truce?" he asked, extending a hand my way.

I nodded. "Truce," I agreed, shaking his hand, even as I knew something had shifted between us that would never be quite the same again. And as his warm hand lingered just a moment too long on mine, I suddenly wasn't sure I minded.

"Good," Danny said. "'Cause it sounds like you're going to need a hell of a lot of back-up to handle the client flow coming in." He smiled, a lopsided thing that was pure boyish-charm Danny.

I returned it, grabbing my coffee and sinking into my imitation leather chair. Today, it was good to be me.

CHAPTER TWENTY-FIVE

The rest of the day was a blur of phones ringing, appointments being booked, and new clients filtering into the office, each wanting the "not guilty P.I." to take their cases. At the rate we were signing new clients, I knew I could forget having to fire anyone. In fact, I was going to have to hire *more* girls. Candy and Apple immediately sprang to mind, and I wondered just what the Spotted Pony paid them.

It wasn't until the sun was setting behind the silhouette of the U.S. Bank Tower in my office window that the phones finally started slowing, and I had a moment to catch my breath.

A short moment.

"Line two for you, boss," Maya's voice informed me over the intercom.

I cracked my neck, gearing up for another introductory call, and hit the speaker phone.

"This is Jamie Bond," I answered.

"Jamie," a familiar voice responded. "It's Aiden."

I took a deep breath.

While Aiden and I had spoken several times since I'd shot Veronica Waterston, it had been all business. It was what neither of us had said that had been rolling over in my mind the last two nights. He'd let me escape from the courtroom. Why? What had that meant? And what did it mean now?

"Hi," I said lamely.

"I, ah, hope I'm not interrupting. Maya said you were very busy today-"

"No!" I said, cutting him off. In hindsight, maybe just a little too eagerly. "I mean, yes, we've had a busy day here, but I'm free now."

"Oh. Well, good." He paused. "How about at around nine? Will you still be free then?"

I bit my lip, staring at the speaker phone. "Why do you ask?"

"I just though maybe you'd like to grab a drink."

Honestly? I could totally use a drink. But with our cat-and-mouse game over, there was only one reason that he'd be asking.

"Are you asking me out?" I clarified.

I swear I could almost hear his grin through the phone. "Yes, Jamie. I most definitely am."

I couldn't help giggling at his complete candor for once.

Giggling? Oh, brother. I didn't giggle. This could be a really bad idea.

"Well?" he prompted. "You know, you're gonna break my heart if you shoot me down again."

I took a deep breath. "Okay." Hey, I hadn't had my celebratory lobster and martini dinner yet, and if the ADA wanted to pay for it, who was I to argue?

"Okay?" he asked, a lift to his voice that I had to admit was utterly adorable.

"On one condition," I added.

"Name it."

"Leave the handcuffs at home this time."

He laughed, his voice echoing off my office walls. "Deal." He paused, then his voice took on a wicked tone. "At least this time."

I felt another giggle bubbling up in my throat. Oh, yeah. This was *definitely* a bad idea.

Luckily, before I could make a complete fool of myself, the door to my office opened and Derek stuck his head in.

"Uh, Aiden, I've got to go. Duty calls."

"No problem. I'll pick you up at nine?"

I nodded at the speaker phone. "I'll be here," I promised, then hung up.

"Who's picking you up?" Derek asked, plopping himself down in one of my client chairs.

"That would be Mr. None-of-Your-Business," I replied.

"Ouch. Come on, kid. I tell you all about my love life."

"Lucky me," I mumbled.

Derek grinned. "Okay, okay. Have your little secrets from the old man. I just came down to see how you're doing."

"Busy. Business is booming. The phone hasn't stopped ringing all day."

He nodded. "Good, but that's not what I meant. How are *you* doing?"

For the second time that day, emotion snuck up on me. I quickly cleared it from my throat. "I'm good. I'm fine."

Derek gave me a long look. Then, as if satisfied, nodded again. "Good. You're a tough kid, James."

"Well, I learned from the toughest."

Derek pointed at me and winked. "Damned straight."

The intercom on the phone buzzed. I leaned over and hit the button. "Yes?"

"Sorry for the interruption. It's Sam. Maya's busy on the other line, but there's a call on hold for you. Another new client."

"Thanks." I turned back to Derek.

He stood, taking his cue. "Sam. That's the one with the legs, right?"

I rolled my eyes. "You know, we may have to hire more help. Maya's totally overwhelmed out there, and there's no way Sam, Caleigh and I can handle all the cases."

"Sure. Hire away," he responded. "I trust you can handle it."

I paused. "Seriously? No demands to be a part of the interview process? No need to check out the resumes or bodies?"

He tapped his temple. "Never mix pleasure with business. Too many complications."

"Since when has that ever stopped you from checking out my girls?"

He held up his hands and wiggled all ten fingers. "Look but don't touch. It's the golden rule."

I couldn't help grinning. "So, this 'trust' thing. Does this mean you'll stop checking up on my every case?"

He furrowed his brows. "Don't get carried away. You still got a lot to learn from the old guy."

I pursed my lips and gave him a dirty look.

"But," he said. Then stepped around the desk and grabbed my shoulders, planting a quick peck on my forehead. "You're one hell of a P.I., kid. You make the old guy proud."

I felt that emotion in my throat again, but this time I didn't mind it so much.

"Thanks, Dad."

He squeezed my shoulder, gave me a smile, then headed for the door.

"Hey, Derek?"

He stopped and turned around.

"They all have legs," I told him.

He chuckled and walked out, shutting my office door behind him.

I circled to my chair and grabbed a pen and pad of paper. Then picking up the phone receiver, I hit the button next to the green flashing light indicating my waiting call.

"Bond Agency. James Bond speaking."

ABOUT THE AUTHORS

Gemma Halliday is the *New York Times* and *USA Today* bestselling author of the *High Heels Mysteries*, the *Hollywood Headlines Mysteries,* the *Deadly Cool* series of young adult books, as well as several other works. Gemma's books have received numerous awards, including a Golden Heart, a National Reader's Choice award and three RITA nominations. She currently lives in the San Francisco Bay Area where she is hard at work on several new projects.

To learn more about Gemma, visit her online at
www.GemmaHalliday.com

Jennifer Fischetto, national bestselling author, writes dead bodies for ages thirteen to six-feet-under. When not writing, she enjoys reading, eating, singing, and watching way too much TV. She also adores trees, thunderstorms, and horror movies. She lives in Western Massachusetts with her two awesome children, who love to throw new ideas her way, and two fuzzy cats, who love to get in the way.

Unbreakable Bond is her debut novel.
For more information, follow her on Twitter:
@jennfischetto or visit her at http://jenniferfischetto.com.

CPSIA information can be obtained at www.ICGtesting.com
Printed in the USA
LVOW10s1547300715

448251LV00001B/118/P